MW01164618

WHO COULD FORGET THE MAYOR OF LODI?

WHO COULD FORGET THE MAYOR OF LODI?

Virginia Bradley

DODD, MEAD & COMPANY
NEW YORK

1 2 3 4 5 6 7 8 9 10

Library of Congress Cataloging in Publication Data

Bradley, Virginia, date
    Who could forget the mayor of Lodi?

    Summary: Lois' dream of going to college to study
geology, an unusual field for a woman in Nebraska in the
1930s, is complicated by her parents' opposition and her
involvement in the mental breakdown of her best friend's
mother.
    [1. Mental illness-Fiction.   2. Sex role—Fiction.
3. Nebraska—Fiction]   I. Title.
PZ7.B7259Wh   1985   [Fic]   84-24730
ISBN 0-396-08504-0

To Betty, my daughter
who has the heart of Lois

WHO COULD FORGET THE MAYOR OF LODI?

1.

Betsy doesn't like to be pushed more than thirty-five miles an hour, and I was only halfway to Bannister when I heard the *hisst* and then the *plat-plat-plat* that meant trouble. I eased over to the shoulder and got out to have a look. The right rear tire— flat as the prairie.

"Darn it," I said out loud. I knew the tires were bad but I was counting on getting home to my dad's garage before anything had to be done about them. And what a desolate stretch of road to be caught on. Not a house or barn in sight and nothing but the graveled highway in a straight line behind and ahead of me.

The sun had disappeared too, the wind was rising from the south, and flurries of dust were beginning to spiral across the fields. Nebraska hadn't been faring well in the weather department. Everyone said '35 had to be the worst possible year, but so far '36 hadn't been any better, and it was already the middle of May.

Okay, I might as well tackle the job. Sure, I knew how to do it. I hadn't grown up in the shadow of a grease rack for nothing. There was a wrench in the glove compartment, and I got the spare tire off the back end of the car and leaned it up against the running board. It was then that I remembered where the jack was.

"Darn it," I said again. "Isn't that the berries?" I guess I wasn't thinking very straight when I loaded my belongings into the rumble seat of my little old Betsy this afternoon. I'd been in such a hurry to get out of Spring Willow. I was through with teaching, and with the help of my summer job at Ryan's I had other bigger plans for fall. I was anxious to get home and tell the folks, and to tell my friend Dev, too—see if she thought I was crazy.

As it was I hadn't gotten away very early. It took me two solid hours to pack. There was so much stuff, and it was four-thirty before I had that last box of books wedged in and my Indian blanket tied down over the whole kit and caboodle. And now I'd have to unload everything if I wanted that jack. I certainly didn't want to be caught in a dust storm, and it wasn't likely anybody'd come by to help. There wouldn't be many cars on the road in the middle of the week.

I had the blanket off and was trying to unwedge the box of books when I saw the yellow roadster heading toward me. The top was down, and I could see the driver was young and alone. He pulled to a stop across the highway and got out. His hair was tousled and dust blown, but the wind couldn't do anything to spoil that dapper mustache. He had to be the handsomest guy I'd ever seen. I just love a mustache, and boy, you sure don't see any around Bannister.

"What have we here?" he said. "A damsel in distress?" He sounded like a drama coach.

8

As he came closer, my first impression was confirmed. A real collar ad with a tan that looked as though it had been put on with a spray gun and a wide mouth that turned up at the corners—the kind that seems always halfway into a smile.

"I guess you could put it that way," I said. "And I'm sure glad to see you. Hope you have a jack. I got this far but . . ."

"Oh, come on." He spoke in an offhand manner, but he was talking down to me all right. "You weren't really planning on doing the job yourself?"

"Why not?" I said. "I figure if a girl's going to drive, she ought to be able to change a tire."

"You don't even look old enough to drive."

"I'm old enough." He was beginning to make me mad. So I'm only a fraction over five feet tall and I've got this short curly hair that makes me look like a child. I can't help that. "And I could change the tire," I said, "if I had a jack."

"You mean you don't have one?"

"I do, but it's under all that." I pointed to the loaded rumble seat. "It took a lot of work to get that stuff in there."

He walked around Betsy, looking her over. "You not only look too young to drive, you don't know the prerequisites for travel. All your tires have seen better days, and leaving your tools in an inaccessible place wasn't very smart."

"You should talk—driving across the Plains with the top down. If that dust keeps roiling up from the south you'll be sorry."

"A point well taken," he said and grinned.

"Besides, Betsy was supposed to give me no trouble till I got home. I thought we had an understanding."

"Betsy?"

"We Applebys always christen our cars—makes them members of the family—more dependable."

"Looks like Betsy let you down this time," he said. "I'll get my tools."

While he jacked up the car and proceeded to change the tire, I told him who I was, where I was coming from, and where I was going. "And now," I said, "I'm never going to make it to Bannister before dark."

"Bannister?" There was a funny lift to his voice as if he was going to make some crack about my hometown. He didn't, though, only gave me a sharp look and said, "Well, Lois Appleby, I'll get you on your way again as fast as I can."

"Oh, I didn't mean you had anything to do with my being so late. Hope you didn't think that, for Pete's sake. I should have started earlier. My friend Ellen didn't waste any time getting away. Of course, she was going back to Omaha and they were flagging the express for her, but both of us were ready to leave Spring Willow. Most of the time it was pretty boring there."

"No night life?" He didn't look at me—just concentrated on his work.

"Are you kidding? In Spring Willow they don't think teachers should have any fun. And a lot of us gals are just railroaded into the classroom in the first place, you know. We aren't offered many other choices. Nursing, typing, and I suppose you could throw in marriage and motherhood. That's about all. It was just taken for granted I'd go to normal school, and I did for a year. Then after a term in a country one-roomer, I landed at Spring Willow. But I don't intend to stay with second graders all my life. I think as long as you have to work, you ought to do what you really like. Take Ben, Ben Oldham. He's got his heart and soul in farming. He used to talk to me by the hour about soil conservation, crop rotation, and things like that. He just loves making things grow."

"And what do you love?"

I think that was meant to be funny.

"I've got plans," I said. "I've saved some money—not easy with paychecks only nine months out of the year—and I'm going to be working through the summer. Mr. Ryan said I could help out at the drugstore. Then in the fall I'm going to the university. And you know what I'm taking? Geology. How about that?"

He looked up from his hunched position. "Geology?"

"Sure," I said. I was getting tired of his answering me with a question. "And I'm not just interested in rocks. Someday I'd like to work in the oil fields."

"Bravo."

I could tell he was thinking the rocks were in my head, and I was mad at myself for blurting out all my plans. Ben was the only one who knew about them. I had to explain to him why I wasn't coming back to Spring Willow. But I hadn't even told my folks yet. That was the bomb I'd drop when I got home. At least the guy didn't laugh and before he made any further comment I changed the subject.

"Boy," I said, "have I been rattling on. Now it's your turn. With that tan of yours you can't possibly belong around here. At this time of the year we're all pale and pasty."

"No, I'm no Cornhusker," he said as he let the car down carefully and removed the jack. "Almost finished. Record time."

"Hey," I said. "You know I took advantage of you. I only asked for your jack. You've done the whole job. I could at least have helped."

"You did your share. You provided the conversation."

My embarrassment must have shown in my face. "I guess I don't have any trouble doing that," I said. "I'm a person who needs to talk. Even while I was driving along the highway here,

I was wishing I had someone with me. I don't know what I would have done this last year without Ellen. And when I get home I'll have Dev. Devonnabelle. Isn't that a name? Her mother did that to her. Poor Dev. She'll probably stay in Bannister forever, working at the grocery store and taking care of her mother. But she's sure a good friend."

By then the guy had the bad tire on the back of the car, and he took a handkerchief out of his pocket and wiped his hands. "There you are, Curlyhead," he said. "Maybe I'll see you again some day. Maybe some rainy day. You're bound to be caught in a downpour without any protection. Now you keep Betsy on tiptoe. If you're going to Bannister I know you still have some road ahead." He gathered up his things and started across the highway.

"I'll make it," I said. "That was the worst tire. And thanks a lot. But hey, you didn't tell me your name."

He climbed into the roadster without opening the door, and as he took off he shouted, "Just remember me as the Mayor of Lodi. That'll do."

The Mayor of Lodi. Talk about a line. He was right about one thing though. I provided the conversation. Too much of it. I'd given that guy the story of my life and hadn't found out a thing about him. Darn it. The best-looking fellow I ever laid eyes on and I didn't even know his name. I put Betsy in gear and headed north.

And where the heck was Lodi?

2.

Thank goodness I didn't have any more trouble and the miles seemed to clip away a little faster. Maybe it was because I was thinking about that handsome guy, wondering where he came from. But I was thinking about my plans too and the summer ahead.

I hadn't been home in over a month—since Easter. Now that I was going to live there again, at least for awhile, how would it be? Maybe just as boring as it was in Spring Willow. Ben said he'd drive up to see me, and I sure hoped he would. I didn't know who there was in Bannister to date. Most of the gang I ran around with in high school had scattered. Off to the university, back to the farm, even into the navy. I didn't see any of them much anymore—except for Dev Skinner.

I had intended to stop by to see Dev before I went home, but The Hill is out northeast of town, off the beaten track. And it was so late. I'd see her tomorrow.

No way had I been able to make it before dark, and not only that, as I drove through town, I saw that most everything was pretty well locked up. Except for dim lights in the poolhall and the lobby of the hotel, there was no sign of life. Even the drugstore was closed, darn it. I wanted to let Mr. Ryan know I'd be at work first thing in the morning. I'd have to call him.

As I turned the corner onto our street and slowed to a crawl, my little brother zoomed out of the darkness into the beam of my headlights.

"Hey, Losie," he shouted. Buzz is the only one who calls me Losie. That's the way my name came out when he first started to talk and he stuck with it.

"Hey, yourself," I said, leaning from the window. "What are you doing out here? It's late. We got out a couple of days early in Spring Willow, but don't you have school tomorrow?"

"Nah, Harvey has graduation stuff yet, but my school's over." He jumped onto the running board and clung to the door. "And I passed, Losie. I'm in third grade." His grin showed me that that one front tooth still wasn't in. "But where you been? I was waiting for you. Mom said you'd be home to fix supper."

"Mom said what? What are you talking about?" We pulled up in front of the house and I got out of the car.

"I'm talking about supper. We haven't had any. We fixed peanut butter sandwiches, but I'm still hungry." He ran down the walk and bounded up the porch steps into the house shouting, "She's home, Harvey. Losie's home."

Harvey came out of the kitchen with a sandwich in one of his fat hands and a glass of milk in the other. "It's about time you got here," he said. "What took you so long?"

"If you must know," I snapped, "I stopped to visit—with the Mayor of Lodi." Harve makes me so mad sometimes.

"You don't need to make wisecracks," he said.

14

I smiled, remembering "the Mayor," but I didn't explain. "What's going on here anyhow?" I said. "Where are the folks?"

"They drove up to Parker. Grandma Appleby had an accident, fell or something."

"Oh, no. Poor Neena. Is she all right?"

"There's a note for you."

The note, propped up against an empty milk bottle on the kitchen table, filled me in. Grandma Appleby had had a fall. It was a neighbor who phoned. She said she didn't think it was too serious but felt she ought to let somebody know. They hoped to get back for Harvey's graduation on Saturday night, but if they didn't Harvey understood and they'd make it up to him. Incidentally, would I please iron his white shirt for the senior banquet on Friday and Buzz had an appointment Thursday—tomorrow—with the dentist in Redmond. That stopped me.

"How can I go to Redmond with Buzz? I start work in the morning."

Harve smirked. "No you don't. Mr. Ryan called a couple of hours ago, wanted to talk to you. Anyhow he told me there wasn't a job after all. Said he'd explain."

Oh boy, that's all I needed.

While Buzz pulled at my arm, I read the rest of the note. Then I really exploded. "Mom says here there's ground meat in the refrigerator. How come you didn't fix hamburgers, Harve?"

He shrugged. "Mom said you'd be home. Besides you know I can't cook."

"What a dodo. You could at least have opened a can of soup."

"Buzz doesn't like soup."

Now it was Buzz's turn to explode. "Harvey, that's a big lie. You didn't even ask me."

In no mood for a family squabble, I said, "Well, you guys, I'm tired, and I've got all my stuff to unload. Soup's what you'll get or nothing. Get out the kettle, Buzz. I'm hungry too."

I got things started with Buzz's help, and Harve stationed himself in front of the radio and played around with the dial until he found some band music. That's been his big interest since he was fifteen and got that set of secondhand drums. He's got a saxophone now too, managed to save the money somehow out of his allowance.

Music and food. That's Harve. I think he was the one who didn't care much for soup, not solid enough, but no one would have guessed it. Three bowls. Buzz had asked for tapioca pudding and I doubled the recipe on the box. "Especially for you," I said. It turned out, though, that I ate more than he did. I didn't put on these extra pounds with rabbit food.

After we'd eaten, Harve offered to help me unload Betsy. I think he had a guilty conscience. Anyhow we trundled the boxes and suitcases upstairs into my room and piled them in the corner. He grumbled something about my coming home and disrupting his life, and I realized what was bothering him. He'd been using my room while I was in Spring Willow, and now he had to go back with Buzz. I noticed that he left his drums in my closet, but I decided not to say anything. I always had a room of my own. The folks had intended to make a bedroom for Harve out of the screened porch off the kitchen, but when the depression hit they couldn't manage it and the boys had always bunked together.

Buzz helped me clean up the few dishes we'd used and finally went off to bed about ten. Even though he said he wasn't a bit tired, he was asleep as soon as his head touched the pillow. Buzz is a good little kid. Hope he doesn't grow up to be a Harvey.

I was in my room putting away some of my things and Harve had taken his sax and retreated to the back porch when the doorbell rang. Who could be dropping in this late, I wondered, unless it was one of Harve's friends. I was tempted to tell him to get it, but he probably wouldn't be able to hear me over "Bye, Bye, Blackbird." It was easier to go myself. I put down the armload of sweaters I was sorting and started downstairs.

The bell rang again, more insistently, and I shouted, "Hold your horses," as I flung open the door.

It wasn't one of Harve's friends. It was Mr. Ryan on the porch, his hat in his hand and an apologetic look on his face.

"I'm sorry," he said, "bothering you at this hour."

"Oh, that's all right, Mr. Ryan. I thought it was somebody for Harve. Come on in."

"Your brother gave you my message, I'm sure, but Mrs. Ryan thought I ought to come over and explain to you in person. I feel bad about the job, Lois. Things have been very slow the last few weeks. I just can't pay for any extra help."

"I understand. Disappointed, of course. I was counting on the money, but something has come up here anyhow."

"Yes, I heard about your grandma. Sorry about that too. She's been alone up there in Parker, hasn't she, since your grandpa died? Maybe your folks will bring her down here to live."

"Oh, I don't know about that. Neena might come to visit, but I don't think she'd want to give up her house." We were still standing just inside the door, and I finally remembered my manners and asked Mr. Ryan to sit down.

"No," he said. "I'll be running along. I just wanted to explain about the job. I'm hoping things will get better before the summer's over. We'll see. And again forgive me for coming so late. I saw your car turn into the street—when was it?—eight-

thirty or so?—and meant to get over right then, but Doc Byford called and needed a prescription. I had to go down and open
up the store. We talked a bit, of course, and then I told him I
might as well make the delivery to The Hill for him."

Another medicine for Mrs. Skinner, I thought. What now?
But I didn't ask, only assured Mr. Ryan again that it really wasn't
too late. "I won't get to bed for an hour or so yet. It was nice
of you to come."

He was out the door and halfway down the steps when he
turned and said, "You were a friend of the Skinner girl, weren't
you? Back in high school?"

"Yes. We're still friends."

"Good. That's good." Somehow he seemed to be talking to
himself. "Frankly, I'm afraid for that girl."

I wasn't sure I heard right. "What do you mean?" I said. "Is
Dev sick? Was the doctor's prescription for her?"

"No, oh no. It was for her mother, and perhaps I shouldn't
have said anything. Good night, Lois. Don't be a stranger at the
soda fountain now. The least I can do is treat you to a double
chocolate."

I said something about not encouraging my sweet tooth and
waved a final good night. But it was what he said about Dev
that was on my mind. Everyone in town felt sorry for Devonnabelle Skinner, no matter what they thought about her father.
But *afraid for her?* That was something else. I stood at the open
door long after Mr. Ryan had disappeared into the blackness beyond the arc of light from the street lamp. I couldn't imagine
what he meant.

3.

The next morning I managed to pull myself out of bed by eight o'clock. Certainly not one of those people who snaps to attention at the crack of dawn, I'd much rather have snuggled in until noon. But I had to see Dev as soon as possible. During my spring vacation I didn't have much time with her. My family spent most of Easter week in Parker. Now that I think about it, that one afternoon when I did get over to see Dev I wasn't there more than an hour. We didn't even go in the house, just sat out on the front porch and talked. At least I talked. Dev didn't have too much to say, but that wasn't unusual. Surely though, if there was anything really wrong, she would have told me. Of course, something could have happened since then. Or maybe there was no cause for Mr. Ryan to be upset. Maybe all Dev needed was some fun. I'm sure she wasn't dating anybody. If Ben kept his promise about coming up to see me, I'd ask him to bring another fellow along.

I dressed in a hurry and dashed downstairs. Buzz was already in the kitchen with his cornflakes and milk. He offered to fix some for me, but I wasn't going to take time to eat. The two of us, and it took two, rousted Harve out of bed, and he promised to hang around home with Buzz while I was gone. He didn't have anything to do today.

It was a decent morning. The wind was down for one thing and that meant no dust. I might have walked, but it was pretty far. Besides I wanted to drop that tire off at the garage. Danny Petersen would be taking care of the business while Dad was out of town, and he could tell me whether the thing was worth patching.

I'd left Betsy parked in front of the house and you can be sure I checked for flats before I slid behind the wheel.

There was already some stirring in the neighborhood. Next door, Mr. Taylor was taking off his storm doors, and across the street old Mrs. Spires puttered with her window boxes. They both waved to me, welcomed me home. Bannister's a comfortable little town. I guess it has its share of gossips and meddlers, but mostly everyone's friendly. Dev's mother has always been one of the exceptions. She never had anything to do with the folks in town. Mr. Skinner had his business friends, of course, but as far as I know, Doctor Byford was the only person who was ever entertained up on The Hill. Mom said the church women used to try to get Mrs. Skinner to come to Ladies Aid, but they finally gave up—left her alone. I guess she thought she was better than everybody else. A real snob. And no one was good enough for Devonnabelle. It was Mrs. Skinner's fault that Dev kept everyone at arm's length all through school, especially the boys. Of course, there had been Gully Huxton, who wouldn't be scared off. He'd gone out with Dev a few times when we were seniors. Funny thing, Gully was the one person Mrs. Skinner was right about.

By the time I got down to Main Street, it was almost nine o'clock and most of the business places were opening up. Miller's Feed Store, the barber shop, Claybourne's Dry Goods, of course, Ryan's, and even the poolhall. Sometimes I wonder if it ever closes.

Mr. Emmett was sweeping off the sidewalk in front of the grocery store, and I pulled up to the curb to talk to him. He was chewing on a toothpick and he took it out of his mouth and tucked it into his vest pocket before he leaned on his broom and said, "Well, Lois, nice to have you back in town."

"Thanks," I said. "Dev here yet?"

"Devonna isn't coming in this morning, Lois. She called. Her mother, I guess. Say, I hear your folks drove up to Parker yesterday. Will they be gone long?"

"Just a day or two I hope. Anyhow I'm chief cook. I'll send Harve down for some things this afternoon. Right now I think I'll go on up to The Hill to see Dev. Any message?"

He shook his head. "Nope. Just say I'll be glad when she's back. Devonna's a good worker."

"Sure thing," I said, and drove on. Mrs. Skinner must be pretty sick to keep Dev from her job. I didn't stop at the garage. The tire could wait. Instead I turned east and then north again, past the picnic grounds and on to The Hill. Cameron Hill. Dev's grandfather, Ace Cameron, had come out from the East before the turn of the century and put every penny he could lay his hands on into land. He owned practically the whole town at one time, but I guess things changed when his darlin' Malvina, Dev's mother, married Henry Skinner. I don't know exactly how I knew all this—just from bits and pieces. I remember my mother telling Neena that Henry Skinner was the burr in the berry patch as far as the Cameron fortunes were concerned. The Hill was all they had left.

And The Hill wasn't the same anymore. The road to the top had always been narrow, but now it was rutted and overgrown with weeds. The old brick mansion up there in the middle of the sycamores used to be so grand. Now with ragged shrubbery and a couple of dangling shutters, it looked pretty shabby.

I swung into the drive that circled around to the front of the house and turned off the motor. There was a scurry of sparrows and a rustling in the tall grass. A cat, most likely, or maybe a rabbit. I climbed the porch steps, rang the bell and waited. Dev was one of those early risers. I was sure she'd been up for hours. When she didn't answer I rang again and then knocked on the heavy oak door. Still no answer, and I went around to the back of the house.

"Dev," I called. "Dev, it's Lois."

Now that I was here I wondered what I expected to find. Would whatever bothered Mr. Ryan be out in the open for me to see, or would I have to ask? I'd said Dev and I were friends and we were, but it was only after we graduated from high school that we began to see each other a lot. At first I guess I felt sorry for her like everyone else. But as time went on I realized Dev was the kind of person you could trust. For at least two years now she's been the closest friend I have in Bannister. I think she likes me. She sure puts up with my chatter.

I was about ready to give up, and wishing I'd taken the time to stop last night, when the back door opened, rather cautiously I thought, and Dev came out. She looked a little thinner maybe than at Easter. Because she's tall, a good six inches over me, she could use a little weight. Nothing else was different. She still wore her hair in that Dutch bob that I like. I wish I could wear bangs.

"Hi," I said. "I was beginning to think you weren't home." She closed the door soundlessly behind her and stood leaning against it as though she was guarding the entrance.

"Oh, I'm home all right," she said.

It wasn't much of a greeting, but that was okay. Dev's always been low key. It was just that right now I think she was trying to avoid looking at me. Still, there was one moment when I saw something in those big eyes of hers. What was it? Pain? Confusion? Fear?

She was looking down at her hands now as she said, "I didn't go to work this morning."

That was a dumb thing to say, and I knew that she was holding me at arm's length again, just as she used to. Right then I should have told her what Mr. Ryan had said to me, asked her what was wrong, but instead I sidestepped. "I heard your mother was sick. Is she okay?" It was a nothing question. To be honest I had no real interest in Mrs. Skinner.

Dev didn't raise her eyes. "Oh," she said, "You know Mama."

I wasn't sure what she meant, and I should have just asked. What I said was kind of stupid. "I really don't know your mother, Dev. I don't think she even likes me."

"I guess Mama never liked anybody much." Dev dug her hands deep into the pockets of her smock. "But what I guess I meant was that she's had problems—well, for three years now. You know that."

Of course, I knew. Everyone in Bannister knew about Mrs. Skinner's breakdown. I remember my mother saying, "Poor woman, she's taken to her bed. About the only thing she could do, I guess. Except for her daughter and possibly Clay Byford there's no one for her to lean on."

I didn't say anything, didn't know what to say, and Dev filled in the silence. "Doctor Byford ordered a new prescription for her last night. I hope it helps."

"Should I say hello to her?"

"No." The answer was quick, and Dev moved to the edge of the porch as if she was trying to keep me from coming closer. "She's resting now."

I was relieved. I didn't want to talk to Mrs. Skinner, and I'm sure she wouldn't care one way or the other.

I felt so foolish. Here I was standing awkwardly at the foot of the steps wanting to know what was wrong, and at the same time beginning to wonder about this friendship of ours. I was always right there to tell Dev my thoughts, my feelings, my ambitions, but had she ever really confided in me? Well, dog-gone it, I cared about her, and now I was sure there was some kind of trouble. I wouldn't let her put me off.

I was even a little mad when I said, "What's happened, Dev? I'm your friend, for Pete's sake. What is it?"

She started to say something. Maybe she was just going to change the subject, but she was interrupted by a shrill, peevish voice from inside the house.

"Annie, where are you?" Then the back door swung open and Mrs. Skinner stepped out. She was thin and gaunt as she had been for a long time now, and she wore a rose satin robe that was at least three sizes too big for her. That much wasn't a surprise. I was used to seeing her in things that didn't fit. No. It was her hair that was different. It was swept up off the back of her neck and then arranged in soft puffs framing her face and forehead. It reminded me of my mother's wedding picture. Mrs. Skinner's probably close to my mother's age—forty-two. She tossed her head with a kind of girlish impatience. "Annie Bergstrom, I've been calling you." She barely glanced at me and then turned back to Dev. "And how many times," she said, "has my mother told you not to have your friends over to visit when you're supposed to be working?"

Dev was at her mother's side in an instant. Gently, firmly, she steered her back into the house.

It all happened in a matter of seconds, I'm sure. But not before I saw the tears well up in Dev's eyes. It suddenly struck me that the only other time I had seen Dev cry was at her father's funeral.

4.

Obviously Mrs. Skinner was sending me on my way, but I had no intention of leaving. I was not only worried about Dev, I was curious. All the time I was growing up I had nothing more than a nodding acquaintance with Mrs. Skinner. She barely tolerated the girls Dev knew in Bannister. I found out later she wanted to send her to a fancy boarding school—where she'd gone herself—but Dev didn't want to go. Anyhow in all those years you could probably count on your fingers the number of times I was in that big house.

Then three years ago, things changed. During the summer after the bank scandal and when Dev's mother was up and around again, I began coming to The Hill often. Mrs. Skinner seemed almost happy to see me. She'd talk to me, too, sometimes, tell me all about her college days and how popular she was at the dances. You'd think she was still going to them. She also lost weight, went down to maybe a hundred and ten pounds. But she still wore her old clothes, even though they hung on her like sacks. Mr. Emmett had given Dev the job at the grocery and they managed to get by, but there wasn't any money anymore. I think wearing the Nettie Rosenstein dresses helped to keep Mrs. Skinner from facing the truth.

Now, today, it looked as though she had gone farther away from the truth than ever. What had happened?

I was sure Dev would come back out to me. I don't know why I was sure—maybe because of the tears. Anyhow I sat down on the porch steps and waited. This wasn't the meeting I'd planned on. I'd expected to be telling Dev about my flat tire and laughing with her about the Mayor of Lodi. I didn't keep track of the time, but it must have been a good half hour before the back door opened again.

It was Dev, and she came to sit beside me.

"I'm glad you didn't leave," she said. "I have to talk to you."

It was a victory for friendship.

"First of all," I said, "who's Annie Bergstrom?"

It was a few minutes before she answered. Maybe she was trying to sort out the things she should tell me, but finally she said in that soft, even voice she has, "Annie was the hired girl my grandparents had when Mama was young. Here in this house, twenty-three, twenty-four years ago."

"Wow!"

"Mama thinks she's nineteen again, getting ready to go back to college, Lindenwood. She told me this will be her second year. Mama's just slipped back in time."

"What caused that, for heaven's sake?"

"I don't know, Lois. Tuesday night she was in one of her moods—feeling sorry for herself, I think. She said she wished she could be a girl again—that she was happy in those days. But she is always saying things like that. I let it go in one ear and out the other. Besides yesterday when I left for the store she seemed to be all right. It was when I came home—something must have happened during the day because she met me at the door. Furious. Said I'd been given the morning off, but I was expected to be back by one. And where had I been? She called me Annie, of course."

"How awful. Do you suppose she's pretending?"

"Oh, no. I wish she was. I could deal with that. She did calm down after awhile. Now she talks to me only to give orders. Sometimes I hear her mumbling to herself, but I don't know what she's saying."

"I'd be scared to death. What did Doctor Byford say?"

"She'd gone to bed and dropped off to sleep by the time he came over. He ordered the prescription for her, a sedative I suppose, but he said not to disturb her, he'd come back today. He felt sure she'd be all right, and it was probably just a temporary thing. For all we knew she could snap out of it as quickly as she went in. I had to remember, he said, that my mother hadn't really been herself for three years. For now I was just to humor her."

"How can you do that, Dev? She apparently expects you to be here all day, and what about your job? How can you manage to go to work if she thinks you're working for her? And how did you get away from her just now?"

"I'm supposed to be ironing some blouses for her. She's getting her clothes together—for school she says. This morning I did ask her what she did yesterday, but she said it was none of my business. About my job, I don't know what I'll do. I've got to work. As it is, what I make just keeps our heads above water. Mr. Emmett doesn't charge me much for groceries, and Doctor

Byford won't let me pay him. He never has. But there are other bills."

"We'll just have to figure something out," I said, not having the vaguest idea what it could be.

For now, though, putting myself on her side of the problem was the best thing I could have done. Dev seemed to let down a little.

"You thought Mama didn't like you," she said. "I was never sure she even cared much about me. I was her daughter, belonged to her, but she never held me close."

I'd often wondered how it was between Dev and her mother. They were so different.

"I want to help her though," she went on. "I certainly don't want her like this. It was bad enough before. And honestly, Lois, I'm afraid."

That last really hit me. I always thought nothing bothered Dev. She seemed so unruffled, able to handle everything that was dished out to her, going from very rich to poor and accepting all the ugly things between.

"We'll figure something," I said again. "Wish my folks were home though. Mom always seems to have solutions."

"You don't know how lucky you are, Lois. Everything's so normal with you. And you've got a family."

"You can have Harve if you want him," I said. "No charge."

She turned away quickly and I realized it was not the time for my dumb jokes. Thank goodness I was saved from trying to apologize by the sound of a car wheezing up the hill, and Dev said, "That's probably Doctor Byford."

We went around to the front of the house, and in a few minutes the familiar blue Studebaker swung into view.

"I'd better run along," I said, explaining about the trip to Redmond.

"No, don't go yet," she said. "At least wait until he gets here."

"Okay, I'd just as soon say hello anyhow. Doc's one of my favorite people."

Everybody likes Doctor Byford. He probably carries all the problems of Bannister under that squashed hat of his, and people feel they're safe there. The town's sort of his family. He doesn't have one of his own. His wife died a long time ago. I don't even remember her. And they didn't have any children.

The Studebaker finally made it to the summit, pulled to a stop, and the doctor leaned out.

"Well, good morning, girls. And Lois, welcome home. I'm sure Devonna's happy to have you back in town."

"I hope she is," I said. "She hasn't admitted it yet."

Doctor Byford's as old as my dad, but he's kind of wiry. He hopped out of the car like a college guy.

"Now, Devonna," he said, "how's your mother this morning?"

"The same."

"It might help if we knew what triggered this. I'll go talk to her."

Dev gestured toward the house. "Go right on in. Maybe she'll be glad to see you."

As he opened the front door, he called out cheerfully, "Malvina, Malvina, it's Clay."

"Clay?" The voice that came from inside the house sounded puzzled, and the door closed on whatever answer Doctor Byford gave.

"I guess she doesn't know him either," said Dev with a sigh.

"And he's been a good friend ever since he came here to set up his practice."

"Well, let's just hope he can reach her. I'll talk to you later." Dev was suddenly apologetic. "I'm sorry. I took up all the time with my problems. I didn't even ask about you, your job at Ryan's."

"Forget it. Plenty of time to talk about me."

"I'm glad you're home, Lois."

The warmth of her words made me feel good. "Everything'll be all right," I said. "You'll see." That was my exit line. I climbed into Betsy and started down the hill.

I was almost at the bottom when I met Buzz trudging along on his way up.

"Hey, you," I called to him. "I said I'd be home in time to take you to Redmond. Don't you trust me?"

"Harvey said you might forget."

"*Harvey said.* He probably wanted to go to Chuck's and didn't want you tagging along. Well, get in." I pushed the door open for him. "We have plenty of time. We'll stop by the house and have some lunch before we go. Okay?"

We drove along for a few minutes without saying anything. I had Dev on my mind, trying to figure out how I could help her. She sure had her share of trouble.

Buzz broke the silence. "You aren't mad at me for coming out to The Hill are you? I didn't think you'd care."

"No, I'm not mad. I was kidding about trusting me. You know we're buddies. But that was a long hike out there."

"Not for me. I walk everywhere. Besides, I was going to ask Dev if that man found her house yesterday."

"What are you talking about?"

31

"Well, yesterday I was on my way out to the creek to catch polliwogs and this guy stopped me and said he was looking for the Skinner place."

"A stranger?"

"Sure. Anybody who wasn't a stranger would know where The Hill was. He was from Arizona. Sure had a keen car. Yellow roadster. And he had the top down."

5.

The Mayor of Lodi. It had to be. I remembered his reaction when I mentioned Bannister. Why didn't he say something?

Buzz was talking about his polliwogs now. But I had another question for him.

"That guy," I said. "What did he want with the Skinners?"

"I don't know. We didn't do any gabbing. I just told him how to get there and he drove off."

"If you didn't talk, how did you know he was from Arizona?"

"Because he had Arizona license plates, Losie. I can read, you know."

I felt like a dope. Why didn't I think of that yesterday? No matter now, of course. There was another thing more important. Assuming that the guy had gone to The Hill, could he have said or done something to tick off this crazy change in Mrs. Skinner? One question just led to another. Maybe the fellow had talked to somebody in town. I'd ask around.

We stopped at the garage, and Danny looked at the tire. He

33

decided it was pretty well shot, but he did find another old spare for me. "Just in case of emergency," he said.

I told him not to even think emergency, and then I asked him if he had seen the roadster yesterday.

"No," he said. "But I was on my back under Bill Emmett's truck all afternoon."

The chances were if the guy saw Buzz first and got his directions, he probably wouldn't have talked to anybody else, but I wouldn't give up yet.

When we got back to the house, we found Harve with his sax under his arm and ready to take off.

"I figured," he said, "as long as Buzz was with you, Chuck and I might as well get in some practice."

Chuck plays the piano and since we don't have one they usually go to his house.

"Oh, sure," I said in my most sarcastic voice.

"Yeah, sure," he came back at me. "We're playing a couple of numbers tomorrow night at the banquet you know."

I didn't know, and darn it, I remembered I hadn't even dampened that shirt yet. "Okay," I said, "go on, but don't forget we need some things from Emmett's. I'll leave a list."

He griped, of course, but promised to take care of it. As he ambled off down the road, I shouted after him, "It's the least you can do if you want to eat."

Eat. The cue word. Buzz said he'd like a sandwich—peanut butter, what else? When we found the jar empty—I guess Harve beat us to it—we settled for jelly and finished off the milk. Two more things to put on the list.

Redmond is north of us about twenty miles or so, and the trip to the dentist was uneventful. No flats. Buzz had knocked out that one front baby tooth when he was four and there was still no sign of the new one, but Doctor Vernon told me everything was all right. It would come in eventually.

With that good news, we headed back to Bannister.

I probably wouldn't call Dev until evening, but at least there was something to tell her. It looked as though her mother had a caller yesterday, a good looking guy in a yellow roadster with Arizona license plates. Also, both Buzz and I had seen and talked to him even though we might be the only ones. Now add all that up and you have—absolutely nothing.

"Buzz," I said, "let's stop at Ryan's. I'll treat you to an ice-cream cone."

He didn't need any persuasion. "Gee, Losie," he said, "I'm sure glad you're going to be home for the summer."

Of course, I had another reason for stopping at the drugstore. It would give me a chance to talk to Mr. Ryan. I had a feeling he'd seen Mrs. Skinner last night and I wanted to hear what he had to say about it.

Ryan's Drugstore is at the main intersection of town and it's an eye-catcher. Built with the same red brick as the Skinner house, it's aged a little better. The hign, arched entrance is on the corner, which means that the windows on either side of the door look out on different streets. It always seemed to me that good old Ryan's, with its wide view of the town, had everything under control.

Back in pre-Prohibition days it had been a saloon with swinging doors and dark green window shades that were always pulled down. I was just a little kid when it was closed, and it stayed empty for quite awhile before Mr. Ryan came here from Kearney and turned the place into a drugstore. Some folks were so against drink, it was a long time before they'd even go in. Mrs. Spires held out for years—sent her daughter over to Winona for all her prescriptions. "Those swinging doors may be gone," she used to say, "but the devil is still in that building."

Of course, I'd never been inside when it was a saloon, but by the time I was in high school, Ryan's was our favorite hangout. We all knew that that beautiful soda fountain had been the old bar, and we liked the idea. The devil didn't bother us.

Today, Ryan's corner was quiet, and I parked right in front of the Main Street window. We found Mr. Ryan busy behind the fountain, and he greeted us with a broad smile.

He's a nice man. I don't think he has an unkind bone. If Doctor Byford has Bannister's problems under his hat, Mr. Ryan has its kids in his big freckled hands.

"I saw you coming, Lois," he said. "I'm glad you understand about the job, and here's the soda I promised." He put not one, but two, tall icy glasses on the polished oak counter. "And one for you, Buzz," he said. "On the house."

My brother's face was aglow with worship. "Gee, thanks, Mr. Ryan," he said. Buzz doesn't get sodas too often. He usually has to settle for five-cent cones.

I added my thanks with no mention of calories. Then after a moment of enjoyment, I said in a low voice, "I went up to the Skinners this morning."

"Good," said Mr. Ryan. "Is your friend all right?"

"Well, sure, she's okay, but . . ." I interrupted myself. "Did you see her mother last night? Or was she still asleep?"

"I saw her. In fact, she was the one who came to the door. I didn't go in, but I talked to her—or tried to. She was very strange. Didn't seem to know me and kept saying, 'It was true . . . true.'"

36

"What was true?"

"I haven't the faintest idea."

I hesitated, then decided I might as well tell him how the morning had gone and exactly what the situation was on The Hill. I asked him about the roadster too, had he seen it?

Mr. Ryan shook his head. No, he hadn't seen the yellow car, and about the rest, I guess he was just as puzzled and as curious as I was. "Does Devonna have any relatives near here?" he said. "I don't know the Skinners too well."

"Who does? But Dev's never talked about aunts or uncles. I don't think there is anybody."

"Thank goodness Doc Byford seems to be pretty close to them. At least Devonna has him to turn to."

I caught myself bristling. "She has me too, Mr. Ryan."

"But you girls shouldn't have to worry about things like this." He shook his head again. "If Mrs. Skinner's living in the past as you say, do you suppose there's any importance to what she kept repeating about something being true?"

"I don't know. I'll ask Dev."

Buzz had slurped up the last of his soda, and he climbed down off the stool. "That was good, Mr. Ryan. Thanks. I'll meet you outside, Losie."

"Sure. I'll be right along." There was one more thing I wanted to find out. "Mr. Ryan," I said. "I wondered why you told me you were afraid for Dev. No one's going to hurt her."

"No, not physically, Lois. But this whole business is just too much for a girl to handle, even if she does have you. Let me know if there's anything I can do, without intruding. Come in anytime."

When I got outside, Buzz was waiting in the car and old Harve was sitting in the rumble seat with the groceries piled up beside him.

"No use to carry all this stuff," he said, "as long as you're on your way home. Right?"

It figured. If anyone can find a way to keep from using his legs, it'll be Harvey.

For supper that night we had the hamburger, fried potatoes, and some of Mom's canned beans. I didn't bother with dessert. How my mother makes cooking look so easy, I'll never know. When I finally got the food on the table, I was exhausted. We hadn't heard anything from the folks, but they weren't much on phoning unless it was absolutely necessary. I felt certain we'd have heard if the news was bad. Neena must be all right.

It was around nine o'clock before I got a chance to call Dev. I filled her in on the Mayor of Lodi and then on what Buzz had told me. She wasn't as enthusiastic as I was. What good would it do, she said, if we didn't know who the guy was or how to find him. Also she had no idea what her mother's mumbled words could mean.

"Did the doctor have any luck with her?" I asked. "Did he learn anything?"

"No, nothing. She treated him like a stranger and told him nobody had called for a doctor anyhow."

"So what does he say to do?"

"Just what he said before. Go along with her for awhile and hope."

"I guess you'll have to. Anything else new?"

"Mr. Emmett phoned. It's all right for me to stay home tomorrow, but he just has to have me down at the store on Saturday. There's a truckload of canned goods coming in and he needs help in putting things away. Besides Saturday is always a big day. That's another thing I talked to the doctor about. He doesn't think Mama should be left alone, would like to have me get someone to stay with her while I'm gone. I've got my week's vacation coming up in August. I wish I could take it now, but I just can't ask Mr. Emmett to change the schedule. He's been so good to me. It won't be easy to find someone to stay with Mama. She's so difficult. I wouldn't know who to ask."

I didn't say anything right away. I was thinking. I'd told Mr. Ryan Dev had me to turn to. Well, now was the time to prove it. "I haven't had a chance to tell you," I said. "My job at Ryan's didn't pan out. So how about me? I'll be at your house early Saturday morning even if I have to bring Buzz. You can count on it."

"That's too much for you to do, Lois. Besides, do you think it would be all right—with Mama I mean?"

"Of course. You can tell her you have to spend the day with your sick mother. Annie had a mother, I hope. Tell her your friend will fill in for you. Sure it'll be all right. She doesn't seem to care much for Annie anyhow. She might want a change."

That's the way we left it. But I came away from the phone with a weird feeling. Boy, what had I gotten myself into? A whole day with a woman as old as my mother who thinks she's nineteen and heading back to college.

At least I had Friday to get ready for it.

6.

Friday. To begin with, Harve rolled out of bed at seven. For the sole purpose, I think, of reminding me about that shirt. I did remember to dampen it last night, and the banquet wasn't until six o'clock. I don't know how much time he thought I'd need to iron the thing. Of course, that wasn't all I had to do. There was the wash. Half the clothes I brought home were dirty, and the boys had stuff too. On top of that I needed a shampoo, and pin curling this black mop of mine takes forever.

Harve had a date for the banquet, and he promised to buy me a tank of gas if I'd let him use Betsy.

"On one condition," I said. "There's something I've got to do on Saturday, and you have to swear you'll watch out for Buzz. Remember, no monkey business like yesterday when you sent him up to The Hill. And if the folks don't get home, you'll have to fix something to eat, at least for the two of you. I'll be here in time to get us to the graduation, but that's all."

"You drive a hard bargain," he said, "but okay, it's a deal."

He even thanked me. This date of his was special, I guess.

Twyla Erickson. She'd tranferred to Bannister High only a couple of months ago. Her father is our new minister, and Harve said he felt sorry for the girl because she'd been in three different schools in four years. Don't kid me. Harve wouldn't date anybody just to be a good Joe. Twyla's a doll—paper, maybe—but a doll. I'd seen her when I was home at Easter.

I didn't talk to Dev all day. It wasn't only that I was busy. Given half a chance I might have welshed on my agreement. And I tried not to think too much about Mrs. Skinner. When I did think about her, I made it a point to look on the bright side. Maybe I could get more out of her than Dev had. If we could find out who the Mayor of Lodi was, we'd have something to work on.

After Harve left at five-thirty, Buzz and I had a quick supper and then walked down to the movie. It was Harold Lloyd in *The Milky Way,* and I figured I could splurge just once for Buzz before I locked up my savings for the summer. Buzz is a lot of fun to take to a picture show, especially if it's something funny. He just sits there and chortles.

We were back at the house by nine-thirty and listened to the radio awhile. There wasn't much on but music and when Buzz started yawning, I sent him off to bed. I waited up for Harve. I knew the girls would probably have to be in by eleven, but I also knew that the fellows always horsed around after they dropped off their dates. It was about one when the car pulled up in front. With Betsy home safe I went upstairs.

There was still time for a good five hours sleep, but I bet I heard every tick of my Baby Ben until the alarm went off.

It was a little before eight when I finally left the house. The boys weren't up yet, which was just as well. I had told them where I was going but not why, and I didn't want their questions. I had questions of my own, and in the time it took me to get to The Hill they loomed up wanting to be answered. With my drugstore job down the drain, where would I get enough money to go to school? I'd saved as much as I could. It was a good thing I hadn't bought that pony coat last winter even if I did freeze. But if there wasn't enough money, what then? Now I didn't even have a teaching job for fall. Well, I still had Dad. He was sure to be proud that I wanted to go on to the university. He'd help me. Anyhow I shouldn't complain. At least I wasn't in Dev's shoes.

She met me at the front door and explained that Mr. Emmett would pick her up. "He always sees to it that I get to work and back," she said. "It sure is good of him."

"How were things yesterday?" I asked.

"Just the same. She spends most of her time upstairs. She's done that for a long while, and now that she's Malvina Cameron she wants all of her meals in her room. I don't know why. It's a nuisance, but it saves having to make conversation. Incidentally, you don't have to worry about her breakfast this morning. I fixed it."

"Dev," I said, "have you tried to tell her you aren't Annie—that you're her daughter?"

"Of course I have. I did that way back at the beginning. She seemed to think Annie was playing games with her."

"Yeah, I guess that's what she would think."

"Then after you told me about that fellow, I asked her yesterday right out if a young man had been here to see her. She stalked from the room with no answer at all. After that I didn't try. Sometimes, I wonder what's the use. And look, Lois, I still don't know if your coming here will work. We'll see. I'll be back no later than six. If it gets too bad, call me and I'll manage to make it earlier."

But when we went upstairs it looked as though things would be all right. Mrs. Skinner smiled at me—actually smiled.

Dev said, "This is Lois. She's going to take my place today. I know you'll like her."

I noticed Dev avoided saying "Mama," but she wasn't acting the servant either.

"Lois?" said Mrs. Skinner and I thought I saw a flash of recognition in her eyes. If I did it didn't last long. "Lois," she said again, and now my name came out like a compliment. "Well, there are buttons to replace on my winter coat, and the hem is out of my dark blue skirt. I hope Lois is better with a needle than you are, Annie."

I started to object, but Dev said, "I'm sure Lois is better than I am at everything."

There was a touch of bitterness in her voice, and she edged out of the room with only a nod to me.

I was alone with this strange woman. I wanted to shake her, tell her to knock it off. But, of course, I didn't. I just waited meekly while she pulled a heavy wool coat and a gabardine skirt from the closet. Since skirts this year are down around our ankles, they're not much shorter than they would have been in her school days, but, of course, the styles aren't the same. It didn't seem to faze her. She handed me a sewing box and told me I would know what to do.

"I've some letters to write," she said. "I won't need anything until lunch."

Up to this moment she had sounded like the Mrs. Skinner I

knew, matronly, stern, but all at once she seemed to throw off the years. "And for lunch," she said, with girlish sparkle, "let's have shrimp. Father has them sent in, you know. From someplace. I don't remember where. Yes, let's have fresh shrimp."

Shrimp. Wow! If Father had them sent in, they sure wouldn't be fresh by now. It was weird the way Dev's mother was this crazy mixture of woman and schoolgirl. Well, Dev had said that trying to bring her back to reality had only caused trouble. I might as well go along. No use both of us being in hot water. I gathered up the sewing and took it downstairs to the little sunroom off the kitchen.

There really were buttons needed on the coat, and I found some beautiful bone ones in the box. I am pretty good with a needle, I guess. I love to sew. I was even thinking how easy it would be to take in some of those outsize clothes so that she wouldn't look so tacky. All morning, though, I worried about that shrimp business. There was about as much chance of giving Malvina Cameron fresh shrimp for lunch as there was of inviting Eleanor Roosevelt to join us.

By noon I had an idea, and when things were ready I fixed a tray with a linen cloth and napkin and climbed the stairs. If she had ever really written letters, she had finished with them and was lying down. "Not asleep," she said, "just resting."

"The shrimp didn't come," I announced boldly, "and I've taken the liberty of making a substitution. I hope you like it."

"Oh," she said in disappointment, but she smiled at me again as she sampled my mother's favorite tuna casserole. "This is good—even better."

I won that round, but later when I went back for the tray, I saw that she had barely touched the food. It was no wonder she

44

was so thin. She ate like a bird, which explained why she had so little energy and spent so much time "resting." That was another thing, like the clothes, that she didn't seem to be aware of.

I'd decided to keep my mouth shut until I felt on safe ground, but since things had gone pretty well, I was dying to ask some questions.

"Annie didn't tell me your folks were gone," I said. "Where are they?"

"Who knows?" She lifted her shoulders in a gesture of indifference. "Traveling, I suppose. They do that. But I don't mind being here in the house by myself. I don't mind at all."

"I suppose not," I said, keeping up the masquerade. "Especially since you're so busy getting ready for school."

"Yes," she said, and her eyes glazed over a little.

I didn't want to lose the thread. "Golly," I said, "I have always wanted to go away—really away—to school. It must be nice to make new friends."

"Oh, it is." She nodded enthusiastically. "I have a very dear friend at Lindenwood. Cora. She's engaged and I don't know where she'll live after she leaves school and gets married. Her fiancé loves adventure and foreign lands. She could wind up most anywhere. I never want to lose track of her, though." Suddenly she reached out and touched my hand with an odd tenderness. "Maybe someday, Lois, you can—go away to school I mean."

This was more than I'd hoped for, and I took a plunge. "By the way, I heard you had a caller yesterday?"

"True," she said without hesitation. "And I was so happy to see him."

"Who was he?" The question was spontaneous and I held my breath, waiting for the answer.

Suddenly she seemed angry. "But I've told you. You're acting like Annie now. I won't have that."

I'd jumped the gun. I backed off in a hurry, not wanting a run-in with her now.

"I'm sorry," I said, and with a "call me if you want something" I picked up the tray and retreated to the kitchen. I was just as happy to have time to myself. I cleaned up the lunch things and then called home to see what was going on. The folks weren't there, at least not yet. I hoped that didn't mean a problem had come up with Neena. I asked Harve to be sure and let me know if they got there later.

Once during the afternoon Mrs. Skinner came downstairs, even walked out into the front yard, but she didn't call me. Later I popped up to her room to check on her. I think she was asleep. At any rate I was afraid to ask any more questions. I just hadn't gotten anywhere. The only thing I found out was that Dev's mother was happy to see the Mayor of Lodi. And that opened up a barrel of who's and where's and how's. Darn it. Who the heck was he? Where did Malvina Cameron Skinner know him? Or did she? How does he fit in with all this? I spent most of the afternoon thinking about it. I was certainly preoccupied. I didn't even hear Mr. Emmett's truck. The first thing I knew Dev was coming in the back door.

"How did it go?" she asked.

"It went all right, but I'll tell you later. I've got to dash. Graduation, you know."

"Sure," she said. "I hope I haven't kept you." Then as a sort of afterthought, "Just one thing. Did you by any chance bring in the mail today?"

"No. Didn't even think about it. Maybe your mother did. Listen, I'll talk to you later. Okay?"

Neither one of us noticed that Mrs. Skinner had come downstairs and was standing just inside the kitchen. She pushed Dev aside and followed—no, almost escorted me—to the door.

"Lois," she whispered. "You must come back. In fact, I'll see to it that you do. After all I am in charge while Mother is away. Annie will just have to go."

7.

I couldn't get out the door and down the hill fast enough, away from those whispered words—*Annie will have to go.* I was sure glad Dev hadn't heard them.

Mrs. Skinner wanted to fire Dev. Dev! Her daughter! Oh, of course, it wasn't really Mrs. Skinner but Malvina Cameron, and not Dev but Annie. This whole thing was creepy, and I wasn't sure I should be mixed up in it.

As I hurried Betsy through town, I argued that it was all right to want to help a friend, but I was beginning to wonder if I could. I was being pulled to the wrong side. Mrs. Skinner was trying to set me up against Dev—or Annie. Maybe it would be better for Dev to handle this thing herself after all. Tomorrow she should tell her mother again what was real. No matter if there was an ugly scene. Something ought to be done.

I tried to turn my mind to saner thoughts. There'd been no word from Harve. I guess the folks weren't going to make it. Too bad. And I'd have to step on it to get the boys to the au-

48

ditorium in time. Still, Dev was so right when she said I was lucky. I did have a family, and everything was normal. Home was a comfortable place, and right now I was glad to get there.

Then I opened the front door and was almost bowled over by a perfectly awful smell.

"Harvey," I shouted. "What's burning?" I followed my nose to the kitchen and gasped. The whole stove top was covered with a creamy brown crust, and the sink was piled with dirty pots and pans and dishes. How could they make such a mess?

"Harvey Appleby!" I shouted again. "What's been going on here?"

Buzz slid down the banister and landed in a heap in the front hall. He hadn't even begun to get ready.

"Buzz," I said. "Why aren't you dressed? Look at you. You haven't even had your bath."

"Can't go," he said, apparently not feeling too bad about it. "Can't find my good shoes."

"That's nonsense. Did you look in the back of the closet? Or better yet, under your bed? That's probably where they are."

"Nope. I looked both those places."

"Well, you'll go to Harve's graduation, young man, if you have to go barefoot. There's no time for a bath now. I've got to use the shower myself. But you get yourself upstairs, wash your face and those filthy hands. I'll inspect. Now where's Harve and what happened in the kitchen?"

I'm used to dealing with second graders. They mind me, and Buzz is no exception. Already on his way to do what I told him, he called back over his shoulder, "Ask Harvey about the mess. He made it."

As if on cue, Harve appeared at the top of the stairwell. "It was Buzz's fault. If he hadn't wanted cocoa. The darn stuff boiled over while I was frying the eggs."

"But there are a million pans in the sink."

"Well, I had to get a second one—bigger—for the cocoa, and then there was one for bacon and . . ."

"Skip it," I said. "But you might have cleaned things up a little."

He ignored that. Instead he gave me his martyr pitch. "Hey, Lois, I'm graduating tonight. Besides I was doing you a favor."

"Okay, but I can't do anything about it now either. It'll have to wait until we come home. At least you're dressed."

"Except I can't tie my tie. Can you do it for me?"

"How would I know how to tie a man's tie? Get Buzz. Dad was teaching him last time I was home." I headed for my bedroom, but Harve had another little surprise for me.

"The program begins at eight," he said, "but remember I've got to be there by seven-thirty."

"Oh, Harve, why didn't you tell me that yesterday. It's almost seven now. You'll just have to keep your shirt on. I'll hurry. And Buzz," I raised my voice to reach him over the splashing water, "get out of the bathroom as soon as you can."

I counted to ten like they tell you, and then to twenty, as I laid out Buzz's clothes and hunted for his shoes. I found them in the hamper. Don't ask me why they were there. Then after the threatened inspection, I told Buzz he was on his own.

When I was finally ready to step into the shower, I heard Harve yell, "Holy Moley!"

I couldn't ignore the panic in his voice. "Now what?" I yelled back through the closed door.

"My cap and gown. They don't fit."

"Harve, that's the last straw. You should have checked them out earlier."

"Why? They took all the measurements. You'd think you could trust somebody."

I wasn't sure what I could do, but I threw on my robe and went into the boys' room. Harve's one of the tallest guys in his class. Sometimes I think we can't possibly be related. Besides he's broad, and there he was in a gown that hit him well above the knees and pulled at the shoulders. The mortarboard, instead of hugging his forehead, was perched ridiculously on top of his pompadour. He looked like Happy Hooligan.

"Where's the box?" I said, and when I found it I groaned. "Oh, for goodness sake. These are Chuck's. His name's right on the cover. Call him. See if he has your stuff. You must have mixed them up."

Another hurdle, and I went into the bathroom again and closed—no, slammed—the door. The whole day had been grim.

This time I managed to get almost dressed before Harve yelled again.

"Hey, Lois! Guess what? The folks just drove up. They're home."

It was too good to be true, but I looked out my front window to see there was no mistake. The old Dodger was out there all right. Nothing could have been more welcome. I stepped into my white pumps and dashed downstairs.

Harve met me in the hall. "Now," he said, "I'll take your car and go on. Right?"

"Can't you wait just one minute?" I said, and from the porch steps I watched my mother and father helping someone out of the back seat. Neena. Good. They'd brought her back with them.

Poor little Neena with her right arm in a cast from her fingers to her neck.

"Hello, Neena," I called. "What did you do to yourself?"

There certainly wasn't anything wrong with her legs. She shrugged off my folks' help and came up the walk.

"Don't you laugh, Lois Appleby," she said. "Don't you dare laugh. Someday you'll be a granny and trip over your good intentions."

"Not a chance. At least for the granny bit. I've just decided I'm not even going to be a mother. Come on in and tell me what happened."

While Mom and Dad were getting the bags out of the trunk, I took Neena's good arm—she isn't any taller than I am—and walked with her up the steps and into the house.

The boys greeted her and then Harve urgently tugged at my shoulder. "Come on, Lois. How about it? It's almost seven-thirty."

"For heaven's sake, Harve, yes, go on. The keys are on my dresser." It would be a relief to have him out of the house.

The folks struggled through the front door with the luggage, and my father said, "Hi, Kitten," and gave me a peck on the cheek.

"Well," said my mother, taking off her hat and surveying the living room as though she'd been away for months. "I'm glad we got back in time. I was afraid there for awhile we wouldn't make it. But your father was determined. Harvey's graduation is special for him. Now, let's see what we can do to get organized. Mother Appleby, you'll take Lois's room, and Lois you can bunk on the daybed in the sunporch. Thank goodness for warm summer weather."

Neena flared. "Oh, now I'm not going to put Lois out. I can bunk on the porch as well as she can."

"Neena." I patted her arm. "You know you'll have to mind my mother when you're here. She controls the beds. And look, I hadn't really settled in anyhow. I'm a transient."

Since that was the way it was to be, Dad carried the suitcases upstairs while my mother turned to me. "And a welcome home to you, Lois. I'm sorry we weren't here to greet you properly. Thanks for taking over for me."

I was a little embarrassed and told her she'd better not thank me until she had a look in the kitchen. I'd explain later. As usual Buzz was my champion, saying it wasn't my fault.

Mom laughed and said, "If it's that bad, I certainly won't look now."

It was Neena who checked her watch and said, "There's no time anyhow. We'd better hurry if we're going to the school."

"Mother Appleby," said Mom, "are you sure you feel up to going? Harve will understand."

"Of course, I'm going. I told you I planned to come down on the bus and surprise you. Now that I'm here, I wouldn't let a little thing like a broken arm keep me away."

Boy, I sure hope I'll be like Neena when I'm her age. It's hard for me to believe she's my grandmother—anybody's grandmother. She's something. Needless to say, we all went off to see Harve launched into the world.

The ceremony brought back a lot of memories, good and bad. The Reverend Mr. Erickson, Twyla's father, was the speaker. He's a colorless little man with a receding chin and sparse hair combed carefully over the bald spot on top of his head, but he had a pleasant voice, not strong but honest.

He started off by saying how happy he was to be able to bring his family here to the Plains where values were sound and people looked you straight in the eye. He followed that with all the usual things about milestones in life and helping to shape the future of the country. "We are beginning to rise out of the depression, and we trust there will be a better time ahead. But all of us, even this class of '36, can recall the dark days when the banks closed and everyone was in a panic."

He didn't know how well some of us did remember. The class of '33 at a graduation pretty much like this one, everyone sitting straight and somber listening to words of hope and promise and none of us daring to look at the empty chair in the back row. Dev Skinner's chair. The minister's voice brightened as he went on, but I didn't hear anything else he said.

I was jolted back to the present when Mr. Farrell, the superintendent, came out on the stage to hand out the diplomas. Naturally, he had to say a few words too, praising the class in general and then singling out a few by name, commending them on their contributions to the school. When he said Bannister High would miss the musical talent of Harvey Appleby and Charles Kline, I admit I was impressed. And Harvey looked nice. He really did. He and Chuck had straightened out the mix-up with the caps and gowns and . . . well . . . Harvey just looked nice.

Finally the program was over. The class sang the school song and filed back out the way they had come. When we found Harve in the crowd out in front of the auditorium, I told him he could use Betsy the rest of the evening. It was sort of a graduation present. I'd planned on buying him something, but now I just couldn't spare the money. Anyhow I knew he had a date and having the car was more important than anything else I could possibly have given him.

The rest of the family piled into the Dodger and we started home.

"I don't mind telling you, I'm bushed," I said. "I could go to sleep standing up."

The others admitted they, too, had had a long day, and Buzz curled up with his head on Neena's lap and closed his eyes.

Since it was Saturday the town wasn't yet wrapped up for the night. Ryan's would probably stay open until after midnight, a special concession. No matter what the kids planned in celebration, part of the evening would be spent at the corner hangout. As we drove by I noticed the reception committee had already gathered—the juniors and sophomores who hadn't been at the commencement. On second glance I saw someone sitting up at the fountain talking to Mr. Ryan who didn't quite fit in with the school crowd—but someone who looked very familiar.

"Hey," I said, "that's Ben Oldham. What's he doing here?"

"You mean your young man from Spring Willow?" said my dad. And my mother, leaning around his shoulder to get a better look, said, "Are you sure?"

"Oh, it's Ben all right. I couldn't mistake those broad shoulders and the sandy hair. Let me out, Dad, if you don't mind. Ben'll see that I get home."

Dad had pulled to the curb even before I asked, and when the car stopped, Buzz raised his head. "But you said you were tired, Losie, tired enough to . . ."

"That, little buddy," I said, not letting him finish, "was when there wasn't anything better to do. Someday you'll understand."

8.

"I won't be late," I called over my shoulder as I headed across the street, "but don't wait up."

The folks had met Ben. Last February. I wanted to come home for Dad's birthday, and we were in the middle of a sleet-snow. Betsy didn't have chains, and I was a little afraid to tackle the highway. Ben came to the rescue—volunteered to drive me up in his father's car. Although we made the trip to Bannister and back the same day, a Sunday, and there wasn't much time to visit, it was enough for Dad to find out that he and Ben saw eye to eye on Roosevelt's farm program.

Ben was only eight months out of Ag College then and was working on the family farm just north of Spring Willow. In fact, he still is. Mom considers that a solid recommendation. The folks knew, too, that I'd been seeing Ben through most of this last school year and they approved. Not that they expected to screen my dates for goodness sake. I'm almost twenty-one. But they still like to know who I'm going with. Of course, I can't really say I'm going with Ben anymore. He sort of belongs to the Spring Willow chapter of my life and I consider that finished.

Still, he was here in town right now, at Ryan's. I pushed through the wide corner door and said, "Hey, Ben Oldham, what brought you way up here?"

He swung around on the stool and stood up. "You, of course. I have only one interest in Bannister."

We both laughed. It was always easy to laugh with Ben. Then I nodded toward Mr. Ryan. "You two have met, I suppose."

"Sure," said Ben. "As a matter of fact when I didn't find anyone home at your house, this is where I came. You did say something about getting a job at the drugstore. I thought you might be here."

Mr. Ryan smiled. "I explained to your friend about that, Lois. I also told him where you were."

"Well," I said, "when you found out I was at the school why didn't you come on over?"

"No thanks. Commencement speeches aren't my favorite entertainment. But you're here now. Let's go. Thanks for the company, Mr. Ryan."

Mr. Ryan offered his hand. "Hope to see you again, young fellow." Then he turned to me. "Is Mrs. Skinner any better?"

"No, I'm afraid not," I said. "Everything's the same. It just doesn't seem fair. I'll be talking to Dev tomorrow. Keep you posted."

As we headed for the door, I saw it was being held open for us. Harve and Chuck and a couple of their buddies were on the way in. No dates.

"Harve," I said in surprise. "Thought you were going out with Twyla. What happened?"

He ducked his head a little sheepishly, "Oh, she had to do something with her parents. She says graduation is a big deal with her father."

I could see he was disappointed, and I didn't want to make an issue of it. Ben made a comment about girls being a problem and then congratulated him on getting out of high school. We let it go at that.

On the way to Ben's car I said, "Seriously, I'm surprised to see you."

"Why? I told you I'd come up. Couldn't wait any longer."

"I was with you just last Tuesday night."

"Years ago. Besides I wanted to tell you I was sorry I couldn't get away on Wednesday to help you load up and get on the road."

"Forget it. I know how busy you are at this time of the year. I'm just sorry I was tied up earlier tonight. You should have called."

"I did. All afternoon. There wasn't any answer."

"The boys were supposed to be home, but they were probably outside someplace. And I was . . . well . . . gone for the day."

"Anyhow, now that you've found me—or the other way around—what do you want to do? Mr. Ryan said there was a dance in Redmond."

"It'll be packed to the rafters with graduates. Sure you want that?"

"Only if you do. I'd really just like to talk."

"We could go back to the house. Now that Mom's home there won't be such bedlam." I explained to him about Neena and the emergency trip.

"Look, Lois, your folks will be tired, and to tell you the truth I could use some food. I grabbed a sandwich before I left home and had a soda at the drugstore, but isn't there someplace where we could get a steak? Aren't you hungry?"

"Come to think of it, I'm starved. I didn't eat anything at all tonight. There's a little roadhouse out west of town. It used to be good."

Ben said that sounded fine, and fifteen minutes or so later we pulled in at Johnnie's, which was spelled out in twenty-five-watt bulbs across the front of the low, shadowed building. There were a few cars parked outside—none I recognized. At least the place wouldn't be swarming with kids. It's off limits, sort of. They don't serve liquor but they look the other way when a customer brings in a bottle and spikes the ginger ale.

Inside it was dark, and I mean dark. Flickering candles in old wine bottles provided the only light. You know how it is when you come into a place like that. For a few minutes you can't even see your hand in front of your face. Of course, right away I had to bump smack into somebody.

"Watch it, sister," said a slurred tongue. "Just watch where you're going."

"I'm sorry," I said. "You should carry a torch or something."

The guy suddenly gave a laugh of recognition. "Well, if it isn't Lois Appleby. So you've come back to roost in the hometown, eh? Well, I guess there are worse places."

My eyes had begun to adjust. It was Gully Huxton. I muttered something unintelligible and moved away from him. I would just as soon not have run into Gully, and I certainly didn't intend to introduce him to Ben.

When we were settled at a small table someplace in the middle of the room, Ben said, "That guy you almost knocked over is behind you in the far corner. He's got his eyes trained in your direction. Who is he, an old boyfriend?"

"Heavens no. He was in my class in high school. Thought he was pretty hot stuff. But even at sixteen Gully Huxton was voted the boy most likely to end up in the poolhall."

"He seems to be doing all right for himself in the dating department. The girl he's with looks like a sweet young thing."

I was so curious. Nobody with any standards goes out with Gully anymore. Without thinking, I turned around. Gully leered at me and the girl looked up to follow his gaze. It was Twyla Erickson. Quickly she put her hand up to her face. I knew she'd seen me.

"I wonder how he managed that," I said to Ben. "That's the minister's daughter, Twyla."

"The girl who was doing something with her folks?"

"Right. The stinker. And for Gully she passed up my brother?"

"It isn't the first time the good guy's been stood up."

"I wonder if her father knows where she is and who she's out with? It's my guess he doesn't."

The waitress came then. We ordered steak sandwiches and cherry Cokes and forgot about Gully and Twyla. I didn't notice when they left—only that they were gone by the time we were served.

The food was as good as I remembered, and while we enjoyed it Ben brought up the business of my not getting the drugstore job.

"I'm sorry it didn't work out," he said. "Does that mean you won't be able to get to the university this fall?"

"Well, I haven't given up. Dad'll help me. I just haven't had a chance yet to ask."

"Maybe you'll be sorry you aren't coming back to Spring Willow."

"Oh, no I won't. Something will work out. It just has to."

"In the meantime, what will you be doing for the summer? Staying home? Loafing and being generally bored? I'll have to take care of that."

"So far there hasn't been any loafing, and as for boredom, you just won't believe what I've been tangled up in."

Without going into the background of the story, I told him about this strange thing that had happened to Mrs. Skinner and about my day with her.

Ben was suddenly very serious. "That doesn't sound like a very healthy situation. You and your friend are coping with this alone? How about her father?"

"Gone," I said without explaining.

"I think it's too much for you to handle."

"That's what Mr. Ryan says, and to tell you the truth, I'm doing no good at all. I'd be better off to keep out of it. I've decided to tell Dev so."

"Sure, you can pull away whenever you want, but how about your friend? What if the shoe was on the other foot? If you were in her place, wouldn't you want to be planning a life of your own? Shouldn't her mother be put in a home?"

"Oh, no." I said quickly. "You don't understand how it is. The doctor says it's possible for Mrs. Skinner to snap back anytime. Something's brought this on, and if he only knew what it was . . ." I could see that Ben wasn't going to understand unless he heard the whole story. I started at the beginning, telling him how Dev's father had been the banker in town, even if it was courtesy of his father-in-law. Then when there was all that panic over the banks in '33, and they were closing right and left, his was one of the first to go. "It was during the poking around," I said, "that they discovered Henry Skinner had been using the depositors' money to cover his own bad investments. Boy, if you think that didn't blow the lid off this town. Skinners were The Family. There was a great to-do. I remember hearing a lot of angry talk about seeing to it that Henry Skinner was put behind bars.

"Mrs. Skinner had a nervous breakdown and she never quite recovered. She just sort of folded up and for the past three years she's hardly gone out of the house. It must have all been terrible for Dev, but she didn't confide in anybody. She just seemed to accept it. But I know she was hurt. She loved her father."

"What happened to him?"

"I'm coming to that. I didn't know Mr. Skinner too well, but he was a big, handsome man who used to joke around with us kids once in awhile, which was more than Dev's mother did. My dad said even though Henry Skinner wasn't much of a banker, he wasn't really a bad man—probably expected to put the money back. He just didn't get the chance."

"So?"

"Well, it was the day before our graduation—the middle of May—about a month after the scandal broke. We were at the school for a rehearsal. Dev was valedictorian. The principal wasn't going to change that. Dev's a smart girl. Anyhow, she had just stepped up to the podium when Doctor Byford came to the auditorium to get her. Mr. Skinner had just shot himself."

9.

Ben gave a low whistle. "Rough," he said. "So Dev feels this is a family problem and she ought to handle it. I guess I can understand that. The doctor will do what he can I'm sure, and even Mr. Ryan. He seems to be a good sort. And it's none of my business, Lois, but I think you're going to have to hang in there too. Dev needs you."

It upset me to have Ben say that after I'd just told him I'd decided to stay out of it, that Dev would have to get along without me.

"Well," I said, "I didn't really want a lecture on my obligations. I was just proving to you that I hadn't been bored."

"Sorry," he said. "I told you it was none of my business."

"Anyhow, tomorrow's Sunday. Dev will be at home. Maybe she'll get everything ironed out. Let's talk about something else to brighten up the night. Tell me what you've been up to since Tuesday."

It doesn't take much to get Ben started on his favorite subject, the farm. "Things are pretty much routine right now," he said. "The spring planting's taken care of, and the winter wheat ripens a little each day. It's dry though. I sure hope we're not in for another summer like '34." He hesitated a minute, and then he smiled. "There is one thing that might be really good news. Last night Dad was talking about moving into town in the fall. He says my mother wants to have next-door neighbors before she gets too old to gossip over the back fence."

"Oh?" I didn't know exactly what I was supposed to say.

"If they do move into Spring Willow," he went on, and his face kind of lit up, "the job of running the farm will be all mine."

I had the feeling this was what had been in his mind all evening, that he'd just been waiting for the right moment to share it with me.

"Would you like that?" I asked.

"Would I! I've always hoped I could get a few hundred acres of my own, but this would be just as good. The folks' place will come to me someday anyhow, I suppose. The point is that although Dad always goes along with my ideas on new farm methods—says that's why he sent me to school, to learn more than he knew—I still feel I need his approval before I try anything. This way I'd have free rein."

"I think it's nice to be able to work with your father, in whatever his business, and then take over when the time comes. You can imagine how far I'd get if I suggested that with the garage. Even though I'd love it. I don't mind getting my hands dirty."

"I know," he said with a laugh. "Geology."

"I guess I should have been a boy."

Ben put his hand over one of mine. "I like things as they are," he said. "But how about Harve? What's he planning on doing?"

64

"I don't really know. He's certainly not interested in cars, except to drive them. He says he has musician's hands and they don't take to grease and oil. As a matter of fact, he thinks he's lined up a summer job with a swing band in North Platte. Maybe he will get someplace with his music. Between the drums and his sax he has a lot going for him."

"I wish him luck. Musicians are having a bad time right now."

"Isn't everyone? But I believe as long as you have to work you ought to do what you really . . ." I didn't finish the sentence. That was exactly what I'd said to the Mayor of Lodi. I couldn't help wondering if he was going to do what he liked. Maybe he was doing it already, wherever he was. Maybe that's why he left Arizona. Maybe . . .

"Hey," said Ben, waving his fingers in front of my face. "You're miles away. Come back to me, and I'll give you a penny for your thoughts."

"Not worth it," I said. "Sorry." With all my talking I hadn't bothered to mention the Arizona guy. Didn't want to. It would lead right back to Mrs. Skinner. Instead I steered the conversation to music again, and with a final Coke we toasted the New Deal and especially Roosevelt's W.P.A program, which was aiding all the starving artists.

It was well past midnight, and I knew Ben intended to drive back to Spring Willow. I reminded him that even as fast as he drives it would take him awhile to get home.

He said he'd come again. In fact, he said he had to come again, and although I wasn't sure what he meant by that, I said, "Anytime." It would be nice to see Ben once in awhile during the summer. There'd be other dances around.

I also remembered to ask him to bring someone for Dev if he could, and he agreed to work on it.

Back at the house we sat out front in the car for a bit. Not long. Park with a date more than ten minutes and you've got the neighbors talking. That's life in a small town. Ben did give me a good-night kiss and then he walked me up to the door.

Once inside, I remembered how tired I was. I really could have slept standing up. As I went through the kitchen I noticed Mom had cleaned up the mess. Everything was spotless. And bless her heart, she had made up the bed on the porch for me. I wasted no time getting into it. The day had been much too long.

Sunday morning breakfast is a ritual at our house, and the smell of steaming coffee, hot cakes, and sausage is overpowering by nine-thirty. I managed to stumble out to the table, but I had difficulty keeping my eyes open.

"Morning, Kitten," said my dad. And Mother, presiding over the stove, asked if I had a good time last night. The boys were on second helpings of pancakes, and Buzz was too busy eating to talk. Harve, though, actually put his fork down and smiled at me.

"Thanks for the use of the car, Lois. Chuck and I drove over to Redmond for awhile and then on to Centerville. There was a dance there too. Hope you don't mind."

I was feeling like Lady Bountiful. "Of course not. As long as you treated Betsy with tender care and didn't leave the tank completely empty you're welcome."

Neena, who was already dressed for church, said, "Are you coming to the services with us, Lois? I was impressed with your Reverend Erickson, and I'm looking forward to hearing him again."

"I may not be able to make it in time to go with the rest of

66

you, Neena," I said, "but I'll be along." It wasn't that I was yearning to hear the Reverend Mr. Erickson. I just wanted to see if Twyla would be there.

As it happened I was only about five minutes late, and I slipped into the back as quietly as I could. It was no trick to spot Twyla sitting up in the front row with her mother, both of them in wide-brimmed straw hats and white gloves.

The Reverend himself seemed to be in good form, and his sermon was on commitment and integrity. I wished I could see Twyla's face.

It wasn't my intention to talk to her, but after the service she cornered me in the vestibule.

"I suppose you're going to tell my father you saw me last night."

"Why would I do that?" I asked. "I'm no busybody. I didn't even tell Harve."

"You didn't?"

"Of course not. But I'll tell you something, Twyla. Everyone in town will warn you to stay clear of Gully Huxton. He's trouble."

The relief on her face changed to a pout. "You just don't know what it's like being the minister's daughter. People expect a Miss Goody-Two-Shoes. You can't have any fun at all."

"Depends on what you call fun. I suppose folks do think you should be a model child, and it's hard for you. Listen, everybody has to deal with something when she's growing up . . ." Oh boy, as soon as I said that I thought of Dev, which reminded me the whole morning was gone and I hadn't yet checked with her.

Twyla and I parted with a semifriendliness, and I went on

home. I was wondering how things were going with Dev but decided I wouldn't call just yet. Ben hadn't really convinced me that I should "hang in there." Yes, I'd wait awhile. Call her after dinner.

Sunday breakfast may be a big deal at our house, but dinner is even bigger. We eat about four o'clock and my mother bakes and bastes and simmers until she is literally red in the face. She is also so darned organized and quick, even though I offer to help, I don't do much. I hand her a spoon sometimes, but today Neena even beat me to that.

When we finally sat down, the table groaned under the mouth-watering food. Roast pork, corn pudding, sweet potatoes, an assortment of side dishes, and all topped off with spice cake and home-canned peaches.

We're hearty eaters, but conversation is important too. We talked about the graduation, Buzz's tooth, Neena's accident, and naturally I told about everything that had happened since I got home on Wednesday night, especially what had happened to Mrs. Skinner.

"Poor woman," said my mother. "She's never been my favorite person, but she has had her troubles."

"Well," said my father, "she has a home and a daughter. The daughter will look after her."

"It's Dev I worry about," I said.

Mom shook her head. "I know you feel sorry for Devonna, and I'm glad you were able to help her out on Saturday, but honestly, Lois, I'm not sure I like you getting involved in this matter."

Neena, who hadn't spoken up until now, leaned forward and said quietly, "Isn't that what friends are for?"

She was right. I knew it. Just as Ben was right. On top of that there was something else that was coming through to me. I had expected my mother to have a solution, and she'd offered nothing.

Someone, Buzz I think, turned the table talk to food, and Neena said how good everything tasted. By the time we finished dessert I realized I was uneasy about telling them of my plans. I had been so anxious to get it off my chest all the way home from Spring Willow and now I knew that subconsciously I was putting it off.

The boys excused themselves, Harve off to his drums and Buzz outside someplace. Dad settled behind the sports page of the Sunday paper and Mom and I cleared things away and washed the dishes.

Later, when we were sitting in the living room listening to the radio, just sort of waiting for the "Jack Benny Show," I decided to spill it.

"Okay," I said, "are you ready for my surprise announcement?"

"Well," said my father, setting the paper aside and leaning back in his chair with a smug look on his face. "I'm not sure it's altogether a surprise."

"That's right," said Mom. "We've guessed. You and Ben have decided to get married."

I'm sure my mouth dropped open. "Oh, no, no. That's not it," I said. I was the one surprised. "That's not it at all."

Almost as though to punctuate my protest the telephone rang at that very moment, and glad for an excuse to leave the room, I said, "I'll get it."

The phone is in the front hall, and I was still in a kind of shock when I answered. It was Dev, and her voice was low, urgent. She might have been crying. I wasn't sure.

"I hate to ask you, Lois," she said, "but do you suppose you could come up and spend the night here? I really need you."

"Of course," I said, and I'm sure it was to escape further talk with my folks which made me respond so quickly. "I'll be right there."

I went upstairs and packed an overnight bag before I went back to the living room.

"That was Dev," I said. "She's terribly upset. I'm not sure what's wrong, but she wants me to come up for the night."

"Wait, dear," said my mother. "What's your surprise? Aren't you going to tell us?"

"Never mind now." It was odd how my earth-shaking announcement had slipped to second place. "It can wait."

10.

Way down inside me I knew what had happened at the Skinners, and I didn't feel much like hurrying to get there. Darn it, I thought, as I backed Betsy slowly out of the driveway, everything about my summer was going wrong.

Instead of taking my usual route down through town I went the roundabout way out past the high school. It was deserted now and would be closed for the summer. The building is gray stone, old and weather-beaten, but it still looks important, sitting back from the street with its long wide walk to the front door. There's been talk of putting up a new brick one, but so far it's just talk. I like it the way it is. I had four pretty good years there.

Beyond the school there's a row of small frame houses, most of which have been turned into shops with the owners living in the back. Joe Welty does shoe repair, the Gundersons have a little bakery—fresh bread and pies right out of Selma's own oven. Then there's Goldie's Beauty Parlor. You can get a shampoo and finger wave for thirty-five cents if you don't mind leaning over the kitchen sink to get your hair washed. The depression has pushed folks into all sorts of things to keep the wolf away.

The dressmaker, Miss Harriet Pickering, lives in the pink, vine-covered cottage at the end of the street, but she's no Johnny-come-lately. Been there ever since I can remember and even before that. She doesn't have much business anymore. Claybourne's and Helen's Dress Shop pretty well take care of the women in Bannister. It's easier and cheaper to buy things ready-made. Just the same the little hand-painted sign, *Dressmaking—Smocking and Fine Lacework a Specialty,* hangs as always from the porch post. I remember Dev's mother used to be one of Miss Harriet's best customers.

Circling the town the way I did brought me out on the east side near the Petersen's place. Danny, who's only three or four years older than I am, still lives with his mother and a couple of young sisters. The girls are crazy about horses, and they keep an old mare for riding. There she was, standing out in the field. Pretty boney, but I guess better than nothing.

From Petersen's on to The Hill isn't much of a distance. It wasn't seven o'clock yet and, of course, still light. How many times I'd walked or ridden along here, but this night, because I was taking my time, I saw things I'd never noticed before. The soapweed was in full bloom with its ivory bell-shaped blossoms and the elm trees and box elder seemed to be crowding the road. Their leaves were dry and filmed with dust. I hated to see that and hoped Ben was wrong in worrying about a drought.

We've never lived on a farm, but it was always drummed into me that town folks depend on the good luck of those who work the land.

It had taken me twice as long to get to the Skinners as it

usually does, and when I drove around to the clearing at the back of the house, I saw that Dev was outside by the old pump platform waiting for me. If she had been crying on the phone, there was no sign of tears now.

"I thought you'd never get here," she said.

"Sorry." Suddenly I felt guilty for taking so long. "What's happened?"

"We can go inside," she said. "I've made some hot chocolate."

"Your mother?"

"She's already gone to bed. As a matter of fact she told me not to bother her. Come on."

We sat at the kitchen table, and with a hand that was a little shaky, Dev filled two porcelain cups with the steaming chocolate. Then she told me what I knew she would. Annie had been "let go."

"She says she wants you. 'Get ahold of that Lois,' she said. 'That nice girl you brought up here one day.' I don't think she remembers what day. She has no notion of time."

"Was she mad about something?"

"Oh, Lois, the whole day was a disaster."

"Doesn't Doctor Byford have any advice? You've talked to him, haven't you?"

"He's out of town for a few days. He was called to Grand Island. His sister's ill. Doctor Wilkins over in Redmond is filling in for him, but I'd rather not have anyone else. You know, Lois, I haven't even had a chance to tell Doctor Byford we know for sure someone was here to see Mama on Wednesday."

"No matter about that now. What happened today?"

"I guess what really got me into trouble was the business of the mail. Mama hasn't been interested in the mail for months. She usually just leaves it in the box and I get it when I come home at night, but there's been nothing there since last Tuesday. Remember I even asked you yesterday if you'd brought anything in. I wouldn't have thought about it—we don't get all that much—except that the telephone bill and the electric are both due."

"What are you getting at?"

"I think Mama has been slipping out, taking whatever's in the box and hiding it away. This morning I asked her point blank where she'd put the bills. She became positively livid. 'I have told you before, Annie,' she said, 'you are impertinent, and you go beyond your position. The business of this household is no concern of yours.' Believe me she didn't sound like any nineteen-year-old. She was Mama."

"Oh, boy."

"What could I say except to repeat that I was Devonnabelle Skinner, her own daughter, and she had to understand that. She stiffened and said that settled it. She no longer wanted me in this house. I was to get you, and since she was giving me no notice, she would see that I got two weeks pay. Pay! That's the craziest part. You know, Lois, the only time anything's paid out in this house, it comes from me. She hasn't taken care of any money matters for three years. I just can't believe what's happening."

"Neither can I," I said, "and doggone it, Dev, we shouldn't really be handling this by ourselves. Who else could you talk to? Reverend Erickson? Your mother's a member of the church, isn't she?"

"Not anymore. She hasn't set foot inside the place since we've been alone. Old Reverend Fenniwald came up once or twice and she wouldn't let him in. This new man I don't know at all. I'd feel funny asking about such a personal thing."

Dev may have been wondering whether I'd told my folks what had happened. How could I explain to her what they had said? I simply avoided mentioning it and she didn't ask.

"How about Mr. Emmett?" I said. "You told me he's been so good to you."

"No, please, Lois. There just isn't anybody I want to go to right now. The people in Bannister used to like my father, I think. Used to. But my mother—it was her fault, of course—but you know how they've always felt about her. No, I don't want anybody to hear of this new problem if I can help it, except you and Doctor Byford. Believe me, I'll talk to him as soon as he gets back."

She didn't know I'd confided in Mr. Ryan and Ben, and I didn't tell her. It might have upset her. As it was, all at once she buried her face in her hands and now I knew she was crying.

"Come on, Dev," I said, handing her my handkerchief. "It's going to be all right. I know it is."

She brushed the tears from her cheeks with the back of her hand. "The whole thing is just too awful. Don't you see? She has erased me. It's as though I no longer exist."

"Well, I know you exist, and I'm here, and if your mother wants Lois I'll stay as long as you need me." I blurted it all out in one breath, realizing that instead of getting out of this situation I was getting in deeper. But I said it and I'd stick by it.

Dev shook her head. "You don't know what you're saying, Lois. I just can't let you do it. It isn't right for you to be here like a servant, doing my mother's bidding, watching out for her. It's too much."

"All settled," I said. "We won't talk about it anymore."

Then I told her about Neena's accident and that coming up to The Hill would get me out of the way at home. "The house is bursting at the seams. Besides, let's look at it as though we're both in the same kind of fix. You're without an identity and I'm without a job." I suppose my trying to be funny was out of place, but Dev did brighten up a little. She dried her eyes, and they had that old "I will deal with what comes" look in them.

We decided that I should take the little maid's room off the kitchen. Dev said she might as well stay up in her own room which was in the south wing at the top of the backstairs and had a bath of its own. It was certainly far enough away from her mother's bedroom. She could avoid her. Finally, after we talked a little longer, we went to bed.

The next morning Dev fixed a breakfast tray for me to take upstairs. "It's the least I can do," she said. "After all you'll have to take it to her."

She started to tell me again that I shouldn't be doing this, but Mr. Emmett honked for her and she had to leave. I had told her she could use Betsy, but she said it would only mean another thing to explain to people.

As soon as Dev was out the door, I went to her mother. She was sitting at her dressing table in the rose satin robe, methodically brushing her hair. She had pretty hair, auburn and real long. It had never been cut. I put the tray in front of her and said, "Good morning."

She didn't turn around but spoke to my reflection in the mirror. "Good morning to you too. I'm glad to see you." It was the Malvina Cameron voice, high-pitched and sort of breathless. Her approval was obvious.

I couldn't honestly say I was glad to see her too, but I mumbled something about hoping we'd have a good day. It struck me again that this strange combination of girl and woman thought she was living in 1913 and yet it didn't seem to bother her that she wore clothes that weren't of that year and were also too big for her.

"I told you," she said, with an impish smile, "I would get rid of Annie."

"I'm glad you're pleased with me," I said. "I'll do my best. Enjoy your breakfast now." With that I left, and was I ever glad to get out. Right then I started counting the hours before Dev would get home. I didn't like this job I'd taken on. I had no experience with this sort of thing.

Besides, I felt like a visitor in the house. Most of the morning I stayed in the kitchen checking the pots and pans and digging out recipes. Planning meals and cooking would be hard. I'd keep things simple and maybe she'd be satisfied.

Because of the business of the mail, I made a point of going out to the box to get it as soon as it was delivered. There was a seed catalogue from some nursery in Denver and a circular from Claybourne's. That was all.

Mrs. Skinner did come downstairs about eleven o'clock. She had put on a navy blue wool dress with a white linen dickey. It was a nice dress, though too heavy for May, but good grief, it was like a tent on her. I asked if she'd like to have her lunch in the dining room, and she looked startled.

"Oh, no," she said, as if I'd suggested something against the law. "I always eat in my room." I noticed this time her voice was Mrs. Skinner's, harsh and cold.

Later in the afternoon she came down again. I saw her go outside to the mailbox and wondered if she was surprised to find it empty. Then back in the house again, I thought surely she'd see things that would be strange to her 1913 world, but she made no comment. Of course, she stayed to the front rooms, and the furniture and the rugs and the pictures there were probably as she knew them. A lot of antiques. Besides, maybe it was the same as it was with her clothes. Anyhow, pretty soon she was back upstairs.

Before I started to fix the evening meal I called home to say I'd probably stay on at least a few days, maybe until the end of the week. I could get along with the clothes I had. I'd brought an extra blouse and I could wash out my stockings and underwear at night. If anybody wanted me they knew where I was. I didn't even explain why it was necessary that I stay on. As it was, Mom clucked her tongue over the phone and said, "I don't like it, Lois. I just don't like it."

When Dev came home at six, we ate in the kitchen and, in fact, stayed in the back part of the house all evening. We didn't want Mrs. Skinner to hear us talking. Her bedroom was at the top of the front staircase and she always left her door open. Anyhow, it was pleasant in the sunroom. Of course, if Dev's mother did find out that Dev—Annie—was still there, we'd come up with a story. We weren't going to worry about that now.

"I don't know what I'd do without you, Lois." Dev's words were full of feeling. "I can't pay you back, but I want you to know I'll never forget it."

Darn it, she almost had me in tears. "That's just what you *can* do," I said. "Forget it. What are friends for?"

11.

The next couple of days were uneventful—weird, but uneventful. I felt as though I were in some kind of play with performances that lasted twelve hours at a stretch, and I was never sure of my lines. I was pretty well tied to that big old house too, afraid to get very far away. I went down to the mailbox, out into the backyard, but mostly during the day I stayed inside.

There wasn't any change in Mrs. Skinner, but she'd settled into a kind of routine. After breakfast she wrote letters—or said she did—just as she had on that first day I was with her. But she never asked me to put any out for the mailman. Then when lunch was over, she'd roam around for awhile. Once she sat down at the piano in the living room and picked out a two-finger tune. Nothing I recognized. She also did a whole lot of that "resting," which she didn't try to explain. Our conversation was practically zero, and I didn't encourage any. I know I was the one who believed if we could get her to talk about that guy we might be able to find a link somewhere—something that would put everything back into place. But to tell you the truth, it was a little scary. I was the kid who always wanted to go home when they started telling ghost stories, and this business with Mrs. Skinner was, like I said, weird. Besides if I asked her something that made her mad, she might wind up firing me too. Maybe Doctor Byford would be back soon.

I still felt a little uncomfortable being here in this house and didn't think I ought to do much poking around. Just the same, I couldn't resist the library. That library! Shelves from floor to ceiling with books on art, music, history, philosophy. You name it. There were the complete works of Kipling, Dickens, Thackeray, leather-bound volumes of Shakespeare. Everything you could possibly want. Some of the books looked as though they'd never been read, or even opened, but that didn't surprise me. It was fashionable to have a library, and the Camerons had been fashionable people. Dev was a reader though, and the books which interested her were on the lower shelves, mostly poetry. But there were mystery stories too. Dev liked Agatha Christie. You can bet I spent whatever spare time I had curled up in one of the wing chairs in that wonderful room.

It was only in the evening when Dev was home and Mrs. Skinner had dropped off to sleep that I felt I could leave The Hill, take Betsy out for a spin. I didn't go home though. There wasn't anything I had to go for. Okay, maybe I was really putting off that big career announcement of mine, but still I was pretty tired by seven o'clock. I wasn't used to the kind of work I was doing, fixing meals, waiting on someone.

When Dev came home and after I'd taken her mother's supper to her, we'd sit down with our own food and talk. I need a close friend. It was good to have these evenings with Dev. Although the situation with her mother crowded our conversation, we made an effort to discuss cheerful subjects too. It was certainly no time to air my own problems, and instead I told about Ben's visit and then I harked back to the Mayor of Lodi.

"Honestly, Dev, that guy could double for Clark Gable. I wonder if I'll ever see him again?"

"He sounds pretty unreal to me," she said. "And Mayor of Lodi has a Hans Christian Andersen ring to it. He might just as well have said he was the King of Siam."

"It was a line, sure, but you'll have to admit it was original. Do you suppose there is such a place as Lodi?"

"I don't know," said Dev. "Let's look it up." She dug out an atlas and we poured over the map of Arizona. No luck.

"Let's face it," said Dev. "Unless there was some legitimate reason for that fellow coming here, which will turn up later, we might as well cross him off."

"But I don't want to," I protested. "He did say maybe he'd see me again some day—some rainy day is what he said."

"I wouldn't hold your breath, Lois, but I suppose you could pray for showers."

On Thursday morning, Dev's mother told me that I had the afternoon off, and it threw me. Dev and I had agreed to stick to Doctor Byford's advice, for now at least, about not leaving Mrs. Skinner alone. I said if it would be all right I'd rather take Sunday. I'd already accepted the idea of still being around through the weekend, and we figured Sunday would be a good day for me to get away for awhile. Dev would be on hand if there was an emergency. Otherwise she'd just keep out of sight.

Mrs. Skinner pouted but agreed to the change of days. Then as a sort of punishment I guess, for upsetting the schedule, she found some more sewing jobs for me to do.

That night I was still working at one of them, putting a lace collar on a gray georgette dress, and Dev was cleaning up in the kitchen when we were startled by the doorbell. Both of us made a dash for the front hall. We hoped it would be Doctor Byford come back from Grand Island. He would have been most welcome. But our visitor was the Reverend Mr. Erickson, and he had Twyla with him. Twyla, looking very proper in a sweater and skirt. I hadn't really been able to see what she had on when she was with Gully, but I'd bet my Betsy it wasn't this outfit.

Mr. Erickson removed his hat and sort of bowed. He's a polite man. Mom told me he was trying so hard to be accepted and approved of. It isn't easy being a newcomer in a place as small as Bannister.

"Good evening, Miss Skinner," he said. "Devonnabelle, isn't it? Is your mother at home?"

"Why yes, she is," said Dev, bringing them into the living room, "but she's upstairs in her room, Reverend. She's not well, you know."

"That's what I understand, my dear. I should have come to see her before this. And Mrs. Erickson usually accompanies me, but she's down with a bad cold. She insisted I come along without her tonight, and in fact persuaded Twyla to take her place." He nodded toward Twyla. "I'm sure you know my daughter."

Dev said yes that Twyla came in to Emmett's quite often, and then she in turn asked if he knew me, "Lois Appleby? Her folks are members of your congregation."

"Lois and I haven't met," he said, "but I do indeed know the family, especially Harvey. Fine boy."

So Harve has the minister on his side anyhow. I acknowledged the introduction and noticed that Twyla was watching me, nervously I think. I guess it was an unwelcome surprise to find me here.

Dev said, "Please come in and sit down." She motioned Mr. Erickson to a chair, and I felt certain she was trying to find some excuse for not letting him see her mother. "Maybe you'd like some coffee. It won't take but a minute."

"No, thank you," he said. "I really have just enough time for a short visit with Mrs. Skinner, and then we'll have to go. I promised Mrs. Erickson I wouldn't be late."

"My mother's not always receptive to visitors, Reverend. As I told you she's not well, not well at all. Hasn't been. And particularly this last week."

"We cannot question the ways of the Lord, can we?" he said. The pale gray eyes behind his rimless glasses did not seem to blink, and right then I decided that if this man had chosen any other profession he would have been lost in the shuffle. It was having God on his side that gave him strength and determination. Even as he spoke, he moved toward the wide staircase.

Dev protested that her mother might even be asleep, but he was not to be put off.

"I won't disturb her if she's sleeping," he assured us. "If you'll just show me the way to her room."

Dev looked at me as though to say, "Might as well give in," and I motioned him to follow me.

He must have wondered why it was me not Dev who went ahead of him up the stairs, but I didn't explain.

At the master bedroom, I stepped inside the door and said softly, "Are you awake?" When Mrs. Skinner lifted her head from the pillow, I added, "There's someone to see you."

Oh boy, I thought, what kind of a reception will he get? I

was dying to find out and instead of going back downstairs, I stayed right where I was by the open door. I was really glad this had happened. Maybe just the sight of the minister would jolt something loose in Mrs. Skinner's brain.

Mr. Erickson moved over to the bedside and put out his hand in greeting. "May I introduce myself," he said. "Reverend Erickson. James Erickson, the new minister at your church."

"New minister," she said, and it was Malvina Cameron's voice. "We just had a new minister last year, a Mr. Fenniwald. What did they do? Ship him off somewhere else?"

I saw a puzzled look cross the minister's face, but it was just for a moment. "Reverend Fenniwald has retired," he said. "I came to take his place. I'm sorry I didn't have the opportunity of meeting him. A remarkable man, they say."

Mrs. Skinner sat up and swung her bare feet over the edge of the bed. "I might as well tell you, Reverend—what did you say your name was?—I'm not much of a churchgoer. My folks are the ones. Besides, I'm leaving for school soon. Are you sure you came to see me?"

Again the puzzled look. "Yes, yes," he said. "You're the one I came to visit, and I do apologize for being so tardy in getting here. To tell you the truth I've been busy trying to adjust to Bannister. I've been used to a city. I've been with a large church in St. Louis, you know, for the last year-and-a-half."

Mrs. Skinner seemed to perk up. "St Louis? Well, I know something about St. Louis. All the girls at Lindenwood go there for weekends." There was an excitement in her Malvina voice I hadn't heard before. "And what a coincidence. I had another caller from St. Louis not too long ago. Let's see. I can't seem to remember exactly when it was. Yes, just last week."

84

So the Mayor of Lodi was from St. Louis? Not Arizona? That is, if she was talking about the guy in the yellow roadster. And who else could it be? We were sure she'd only had one caller. Boy, this was more than I'd gotten out of her.

"He's from a well-known family," she went bubbling on. "Maybe you know of them, Reverend. The McChesneys. My friend is Truman—Truman McChesney. Tru. That's what we called him."

Even a name! And while Mr. Erickson was saying something about St. Louis being a big place, I was turning that name over in my mind. Truman McChesney. Truman. Tru. That was what she had muttered to Mr. Ryan. And what she'd said to me when I told her I understood she had a caller. We'd thought she was saying *true,* but no, it was *Tru.* I was so excited I may have said it out loud. I don't know. At any rate Mrs. Skinner suddenly seemed to be aware that I was still in the room.

"You don't have to wait, Lois," she said sharply. "The Reverend can find his way back downstairs when we're through visiting."

"Of course," I said and backed out into the hall.

I would have liked to hear more, but at least I had something, and I was anxious to tell Dev. It would have to wait though until the Ericksons were gone.

Back in the living room I found Dev and Twyla sitting, rather uncomfortably I thought, in the two red velvet chairs by the bay window.

I had told Dev in one of our evenings together about Harve and Twyla and about running into Gully at the roadhouse. I hoped the subject wouldn't be brought up, but my hopes were dashed when Twyla looked up at me and said, "I was just telling Devonnabelle that Gully Huxton told me he used to go with her in high school."

"Yes," said Dev. "I did. Poor Gully. He was—and is, I guess—his own worst enemy. He was spoiled rotten." She paused and then added, "But I liked him."

Twyla gave me a smug look and said, "I like him too."

How could she know that Dev would have liked Satan himself if he'd got past her mother and gave her a little attention. I couldn't let the thing drop there. Twyla had to be put on the right track. "I hope someone can straighten him out," I said, "and soon. You haven't seen him lately, have you, Dev?"

"No, and I understand he drinks too much."

"That and other things," I said. "He never has had a job, and he's leeched off his folks ever since he graduated, and about the only dates he can get around here anymore are with innocents who don't know what he's up to."

Twyla would have kept the subject alive, I'm sure, but she didn't have a chance. We were interrupted by the reappearance of her father.

"Oh, dear," he said, even before he got to the bottom of the staircase. I could see he was nervous. "Your mother gave me quite a turn. I wasn't really able to communicate with her. She said several things that perplexed me, and then she became exceedingly upset because I didn't know some friend of hers from St. Louis. Finally, she sent me away, said I'd better come back when her parents returned. *Her parents?* I just didn't know what to think."

"I'm sorry, Reverend Erickson," said Dev. "I did try to explain to you, but it's difficult. I said she was ill."

"I'm afraid she's more than ill, my dear. Have you talked to Doctor Byford?"

Dev was beginning to fidget. I could see she didn't want to keep this going. She simply wanted Mr. Erickson and Twyla out of the house. It wasn't my place to speak but I just had to. "Oh, yes," I said, "she talks to the doctor regularly. I'm sure the next time you come, Reverend Erickson, Mrs. Skinner will be herself again."

As Dev accompanied the minister to the front hall, I hung back with Twyla. Pressing her arm, hard, I whispered, "And you're not going to say anything about this." It was not a question. Because of the way she looked at me as she followed her father out the door, I knew she understood.

"Oh, Lois," Dev said when they had gone. "It will be all over town now. I hate that."

"Reverend Erickson is a minister, Dev. He keeps people's troubles to himself. It's part of his job."

"It's Twyla I'm afraid of."

"You don't have to worry about Twyla. She's in my pocket. Besides," I said, "we have something more important to talk about. I think the Mayor of Lodi has a name."

12.

"Truman McChesney?" said Dev when I told her. "The name means absolutely nothing to me. Mama's never mentioned such a person."

That didn't prove anything, of course. Dev always said her mother never talked to her about herself and her friends, or about anything else, I guess. There wasn't much between them.

Both of us wanted to hear what Mrs. Skinner would have to say, but I waited until the next morning before I broached the subject, easing into a conversation by way of the minister's visit.

"A very difficult man," she said, giving me one of her stern looks. "If he comes again, tell him I don't want to see him."

Then when I switched the talk over to Truman McChesney, she said we'd forget the whole incident and just clammed up.

I did try again several times, but it was always the same. She apparently hooked the name of McChesney up with Mr. Erickson and didn't want to speak about either one of them. So, although we were pretty sure of the identity of the guy from Arizona—or St. Louis or wherever—it really didn't get us anyplace.

Not that we were throwing in the sponge. We'd just back off awhile. If I stayed away from troublesome questions, things went smoother.

Saturday was Memorial Day, and although there was a parade over in Winona, it was just another day at the Skinners. Mr. Emmett didn't even close the grocery, which meant Dev had to work. She did borrow Betsy in the evening and took some flowers to her father's grave, but she made no issue of it.

By Sunday I'd been on The Hill for an entire week. There was still no word from Doctor Byford, and even though Dev and I didn't really discuss it, she knew I'd just stay on. I decided that now I would have to pick up some more clothes, and I called home to say if it was all right I'd be there for dinner. Sunday. My afternoon off.

Together Dev and I fixed a midday meal for Mrs. Skinner and I took the tray up before I left the house. That way we could keep up the pretense of Dev not being around. She'd just have to keep out of sight when and if her mother should come downstairs. It shouldn't be too hard. It's a big house.

It must have been about three or so when I got home and everybody seemed glad to see me. Neena most I think. I didn't tell about Annie being fired, only that I was staying on so that Dev could go to work just as I had that first Saturday. It wasn't hurting me any.

My mother shook her head and said, "Well, as soon as Doctor Byford comes back he should do something about the situation. It can't go on."

Dad agreed. "The woman will probably stay in that condition. I remember when I was a boy we had a neighbor—seventy years old or so—got it into her head she was seven. She never changed. They finally put her away."

I said I didn't think the doctor was going to let that happen, but, of course, I couldn't be sure.

No one mentioned my big announcement, but I don't believe it was forgotten. I wanted to have the boys out of the way before I said anything, and as it happened the pattern of last Sunday repeated itself. By six-thirty, Buzz and Harve had gone off to their own affairs, and Mom and Dad and Neena and I wound up in the living room again.

I dove right in. "I've decided to go back to school," I said. "To the university."

There was no immediate reaction, and I went on, saying that it would be impossible without some help since I didn't have the job at Ryan's. "I might be able to get work during the holidays in Lincoln," I said, "and certainly I have hopes for a job next summer, but do you suppose I could have a loan?"

Mom tapped her foot nervously while Dad cleared his throat and then said, "But you know, Kitten, Harvey will be going to the university in the fall."

"Oh? I thought he wanted to wait a year—at least a year. He told me that even if he doesn't get the job with that band in North Platte, he has a couple of other drummer spots he'd like to try for."

"Music is a fine hobby," said my father, sounding a little pompous, "a sideline. But Harvey has plans to take engineering, mechanical engineering."

That was news to me, but I didn't argue about it.

"Look, honey," said Mom, "your father'd like to help, but it is Harvey's turn."

"A boy should get an education," said Dad. "One day he'll have a family to support. And after all, you had your year at teacher's college."

"That's right," Mom said. "It isn't as though you're not pre-pared to earn a living."

They tossed their logic back and forth while I listened, and then as though he was winding up the case, Dad said, "There just isn't any money for you right now, Lois. And you do have a job."

Okay, here it was. I set my chin. "But I don't. I don't have a job. I didn't sign the contract."

There was an awkward silence. My mother caught at her throat and my father looked at me as though he thought I was joking. Then his dark brows came together in a heavy frown. "That was a foolish thing to do."

"How could you, Lois?" my mother chimed in. "With times as bad as they are. Maybe you could tell them you've changed your mind."

"But I haven't. I'm not going back to Spring Willow."

"If you didn't like Spring Willow," said Dad, "you should have tried to get in some other town. I suppose it's too late for that now. It's already the first of June."

"Don't you understand?" I said. "I don't want to teach school. I want to take geology. I want to learn about oil. Oil keeps this country going. I'd even like to work in the field. It would be exciting."

My father's frown deepened. "You can't be serious. That's no work for a girl."

Neena, who had been sitting on the sidelines as usual, said, "Hmm. That's very interesting, Lois. You never told me."

"Well," said Dad, "it pretty much boils down to this. I just can't give you a cent. It has to go to Harve. Be honest about it, Lois. You'd spend maybe a year at school and then forget the whole thing, wind up getting married, if not to Ben to some other fellow, and settling down to raise a batch of kids. And that's what a girl should do—raise a family."

Mom said, "You'll see your father's right, dear, if you think about it."

I was on my feet then and sort of pacing the floor. "I'm not planning on getting married—ever," I said. "But okay, forget it. Girls don't have a chance. Anyhow, I'm going back to Dev's tonight. At least I can do some good there." I walked past them out of the room and went upstairs to get the clothes I'd come for.

Neena followed me. "Don't be upset with your folks, Lois."

"I'm not mad, Neena, just kind of hurt. I shouldn't have blown up like that. But Harve is—was—counting on playing with a band. I know it. He doesn't want to go to the university in September. He told me so. They've pressured him into it."

"They're human, dear. They can only make decisions as they see them. Sometimes maybe they're not the best ones." She sighed. "You're right about girls not having the options they should have. I agree with you there. But things will change."

"That's my line, Neena. That's what I used to tell my friend Ellen back in Spring Willow. But I want them to change *now*."

"I know." She sat down on the edge of the bed and rested that clumsy cast on one of the pillows. "If it's any consolation think what it was like when I was twenty."

"I can imagine."

"I wonder if you can." Neena sat there watching me as I pulled things from the drawers, but she seemed to be with her own thoughts. "Do you know what interested me when I was your age?" she finally said. "Law. I wanted to study law. I always felt if women wanted equality they would have to get the law on their side."

"Neena! You always surprise me. Law? And how come I've never known about this?"

"It was a long time ago, dear. I had really forgotten about it myself. Well, almost."

"Did you ever say anything to anybody? Your family?"

I noticed her eyes were sad, but she smiled a soft inside smile. "Once. I told my father."

"So? What did he say?"

"He didn't *say* anything. Just laughed." There was a long pause, and then she seemed to pull herself back to where we were. "Anyhow," she said, "I met your grandfather. I had a good life. I can't complain."

"I'll complain for both of us, Neena." I gave her a big hug and thanked her for just being around. "When the mess on The Hill gets straightened out, we'll have to spend some time together."

When I got back downstairs, I'd cooled off a little. I told my folks I was sorry. "I shouldn't have asked for help anyhow," I said. "After all, I'll be twenty-one in August. I should be out from under your feet. And don't worry about my not having a job. I'll work something out."

I sounded confident enough, but when I left the house I felt pretty miserable. Betsy and I chugged through town as though we were following a hearse. I decided to stop at Ryan's.

Mr. Ryan closes early on Sunday evenings, and he had started to check out the register when I walked in.

"I've been thinking about you," he said. "Doctor Byford called in here just a few minutes ago about Mrs. Spires' prescription. He said he might be gone a little longer than he planned. His sister's out of the woods, but as long as there's no emergency with his patients here he'd like to stay on a bit."

"I guess Mrs. Skinner isn't an emergency, but I'll be glad when the doctor gets back." I told him about the Reverend Mr. Erickson's visit and about Dev not wanting to have everybody in town knowing what had happened.

"I understand how she feels," he said. "You can be sure I won't tell anybody. As a matter of fact I haven't even said anything to Mrs. Ryan. Not that she gossips, but I just figured it was something I'd stumbled on and nobody else's business, not even mine."

"Oh, I wasn't worried about you." I thought of all the secrets we kids had poured into Mr. Ryan's ears as we hung over the soda fountain. Gosh no. I wasn't worried about him.

I guess I really wanted to tell him about school and my money trouble, but I was afraid he'd think I was blaming him because he didn't have a job for me. I wouldn't want that. He's too nice a man.

Instead, I brought him up to date on Annie, told him about my staying at the Skinners and that I was just on my way back there. Doggone it. I was sure down in the dumps. Neena says she buys a new hat when she's low, but I have my own way of chasing the blues.

"Mr. Ryan," I said, "I sure could use a hot fudge sundae."

13.

When I left Ryan's I felt a little better. I tell you I swear by hot fudge. Not that I had the answers to anything, but at least I could face up to what lay ahead.

It looked as though I wouldn't get to the university in September. Ben had told me he knew several fellows who were working their way through school waiting on tables at the sorority houses, but girls couldn't get jobs like that. In fact, he said he didn't know a single girl who was on her own.

So. What would I do? Even if I wanted to go crawling back to Spring Willow, Ben had told me the vacancy was already filled. And Dad was probably right about it being too late to try for a school in some other town. I suppose I should have held onto that contract until I was certain about things, but darn it, I really didn't want to teach. Mr. Ryan said he hoped business would pick up. Maybe by fall there would be a permanent job at the drugstore. I could always live at home, pay the folks board and room, and settle down as a good citizen of Bannister. Like Dev.

No. Maybe I could face up to the fact that that kind of life was a possibility, but I wasn't going to accept it.

Anyhow I was busy for the time being. I'd probably stay on

as the Cameron's hired girl at least until Malvina Cameron Skinner returned to normal. As Betsy and I bounced and jostled our way back up to The Hill, I wondered how long that would be.

Once again Dev was waiting for me, this time on the back porch. She said her mother hadn't left her room all day and she was a little nervous about it. Would I go up and check on her?

"I intended to," I said. "I have to report to her anyhow. Remember I've only had the afternoon off." It was a flimsy attempt at humor.

Upstairs, I found Mrs. Skinner not in bed but at her dressing table. She spent a lot of time there too, and tonight she seemed to be studying her face in the mirror.

"I'm back," I said. "Just wanted to let you know."

She ignored my greeting. When she did turn to me she frowned and said, "There are ugly lines around my eyes, Lois. I've never noticed them before."

I wanted to say she was old enough for a few crow's feet, but instead I told her I knew of a good cream. I started to add that it was what my mother used but caught myself before the words were out. I simply promised to get some for her.

She said she would appreciate that and promptly changed the subject. "Did you have a nice afternoon?" she asked. "Where did you go?"

I told her I'd been home, and then I said, trying not to sound bold, "What did you do?"

Her face clouded as though she was trying to remember. All at once she giggled. "Mostly I've been reading. A book my friend, Cora, gave me. One I'm sure father wouldn't approve. It's a naughty kind of novel—*Madame Bovary*. I don't suppose you've read it?"

I had, of course, but it was better not to admit it. A hired girl on the Nebraska prairie seldom does much reading and probably did even less back in 1913. I avoided a direct answer. "I don't think it's in our library," I said. Actually, Ellen had loaned it to me last year. It had been on her reading list for English Lit at the university. Both of us thought it was great.

Mrs. Skinner leaned toward me as though we were conspirators. "If you'd like to read it," she whispered, "you can borrow my copy."

"Fine. Whenever you're finished," I said. "Now is there anything you want before I go to my room? Maybe a sandwich or something?"

"No, nothing. I'm sorry I didn't even eat all the food you brought earlier. I'm afraid I don't have much of an appetite."

"Then I'll just clear this away," I said, gathering up the tray which as usual had scarcely been touched. "I'll see you in the morning."

She surprised me by saying, "I'm so glad you're here, Lois." And there was a special warmth in the Malvina voice that stayed with me as I went downstairs.

Dev and I didn't talk much that night. She had so many troubles I didn't want to add mine. We turned on the radio, caught the end of the Charlie McCarthy show, and then called it a day. At least Dev did.

I was still thinking about my folks. I felt so sure they'd understand, my father at least. I'd always been close to him. I wandered aimlessly around the house from the kitchen to the dining room to the library. There was no comfort even in the books. Finally I wound up in the living room, where I seldom went. Those beautiful velvet chairs. No matter which one I sat in I could look out over The Hill.

The Hill. I remember pointing up to this house when I was

just a little kid, four or so. We'd be out on our Sunday drives, and I asked over and over again, "Who lives up there?" Then when I started to school I found out that the girl from The Hill would be in my class. Devonnabelle Skinner. Nobody talked much to her, and she hardly said a word except for the teacher's ear. A big car brought her down in the morning and picked her up again at three. One thing, though, from the first grade right on through, Devonnabelle was always at the head of the class.

In high school I was thrown together with her a little more. She was in the Glee Club and on the library staff but, as I said before, I seldom went to her house. There were no slumber parties or backyard picnics.

Here in the red chair I thought of all these things. I forgot how late it must be, and when I saw the headlights of a car halfway down the road, about at the bend, I wondered if someone was coming up to see us. Then the lights went off. Hmm. If there was romancing going on down there, things must have changed in the last three years. When I was in high school we all knew that The Hill would be the perfect spot to park. A place to turn off the motor and listen to Benny Goodman. A place to sit and talk with a date after a dance. And I'm sure some of the guys saw it as the place to run out of gas and try a little smooching. But it wasn't used that way. It was always off limits—Skinner's property. A no trespassing sign wasn't even necessary. The whole town understood. Maybe now it was different.

I watched for awhile to see if the lights went on again. When they didn't I just forgot about it. My own predicament was more important. Up to now I had been waiting for Mrs. Skinner to remember who she was so that I could leave. The talk with my folks today had changed everything. I was just as well off here as back at home. I sort of resigned myself to carrying on with this charade and went to bed.

In the days that followed there was one change I hadn't expected. Time began to go by very quickly. Monday, Tuesday, Wednesday. I don't know where they went, and things moved smoothly with the three of us on The Hill. Nothing disturbed the pattern we seemed to have set.

On Thursday evening Doctor Byford called from Grand Island to see how Dev was getting along. He apologized for having to take off for his sister's so suddenly. Dev told him her mother was the same but that there was no urgent problem. She also told him what she and I had worked out.

"Good," he said. "That's about all you can do for now. I'll probably stay on here for maybe another week, possibly two. Doctor Wilkins seems to be taking good care of my patients."

The next day Ben called. He phoned home first, of course, and was told where I was. He and his dad were busy dealing with the dust storms, but he would get back up to Bannister as soon as possible. I explained that I was staying with Dev for awhile, and he said "Good girl. I knew you wouldn't let your friend down."

I didn't tell him everything. It was too long a story and no point over the phone.

Periodically, I checked with the folks to see how Neena's arm was, and mostly it was Neena I talked to. When Sunday rolled around again and I had the afternoon, I told her I'd pick her up at four-thirty or so and we'd go for a drive. Mom asked wasn't I coming for dinner, but I said no—felt I ought to stay with Dev. That was true, but that wasn't the only reason. I just didn't want to open that painful subject again. I picked Neena up as I'd promised, and we headed out into the countryside.

"Does your arm bother you?" I asked. "I think I'd just die if I ever had to have a cast. Not to be able to scratch or rub, and I'd be sure to get a charley horse."

"It's not as bad as you'd expect, Lois, and it'll be off by the end of the week. That's something I wanted to talk to you about. Do you suppose Friday or Saturday you could drive me up to the doctor in Parker? I don't know how you fit in at the Skinners. Is Sunday the only day you can get away?"

"I might be able to figure something out," I said. "It's too bad Mom doesn't drive. That would be the easiest. But how about Harve?"

"Oh, Harvey'd be glad to do it, but he and his friend Chuck are going to North Platte on Friday. They won't be back until Sunday morning, something about that band. Your father would take me I know, but I hate to ask him to leave his work."

"I wouldn't worry about that. Danny's always on hand."

Neena chuckled and said, "To tell you the truth, Lois, I'd rather not have your father along when I go to Parker. There's something I want to take care of, a private matter. We could drive up and back the same day, couldn't we?"

"Sure. I'll see what I can arrange. But what's the private business that you don't want Dad to know about?"

"It's none of your business either, Missy, but I know you won't fuss at me to find out. Your father thinks women in general, and his mother in particular, should stay in the kitchen and let the men take care of everything else. You know how he is."

That Neena. I had no idea what she was up to, but she was right. I wouldn't pry. "All right for you," I said. "I thought we had no secrets from each other. If you don't watch yourself I'll shift my loyalty to Mrs. Skinner." And I told her how Dev's mother, Malvina, was sometimes almost chummy with me.

"Hmm," said Neena. "Don't forget she hasn't really turned into a schoolgirl. Inside she's still the person you've apparently never been fond of. I wouldn't get too friendly."

"Oh, I don't. I'm careful."

"As a matter of fact," Neena persisted, "I'm inclined to agree with your mother on one point. Doctor Byford may have to do something about that woman."

All this talk led us right into my major problem and Neena, bless her heart, said, "It's just too bad I don't have some money hidden away in the mattress. Your grandpa and I never were able to put much aside, and that last illness of his took what we had saved. But don't you give up, Lois. Something will pan out for you."

"I hope so." I patted her good arm. "Anyhow, I know it's not the end of the world."

After we'd been out an hour or so, I turned back to town. Neena wanted to buy me a couple of gallons of gas, but I wouldn't let her. Frankly, I was beginning to dip into my reserve funds, those I'd intended to use for school. I hated that, but I couldn't take anything from Neena. She lives on a small widow's pension. My grandfather was with the railroad.

When I took Neena home, it was just to the door. I said again I'd see what I could do about getting her to Parker at the end of the week. I'd certainly try. Dev was still expecting a miraculous recovery for her mother. She was sure she'd suddenly be "Mama" again. I'd be free then. Maybe it would happen that way.

In the meantime Mrs. Skinner was the nineteen-year-old Malvina, and although the personality of the woman she had been came out once in awhile, if I was careful about what I said there was none of the surliness she'd used on Dev that first night.

In spite of my conversation with Neena and her warning, I found myself drawn to this girl-woman. Sometimes we seemed of an age, and I reminded myself that in that world she'd slipped back into she would be only a year, a year-and-a-half younger than I. Often she'd talk to me about school and especially about Cora. It seems that Cora was a suffragette.

"Do you know," Malvina said one afternoon, "Cora actually marched in that New York parade last year. I wish I could have been there."

That would have been in 1912, and I found something about the event in one of the encyclopedias in the library. ". . . some 15,000 ladies high-stepped up Fifth Avenue, cheered by a crowd of half a million." Terrific! Of course, three years later the marchers had numbered 40,000, but Malvina and Cora didn't know that yet.

"Also," said Malvina, "Cora wants to organize a club at Lindenwood to back up the suffragette movement, and I'm going to help her, no matter what Father thinks."

Then once in awhile pieces of Malvina's conversation made me think she might be coming around. There was the day she looked at me questioningly and said, "There's an odd motor car in the yard." It was Betsy, of course, and I held my breath, but nothing came of it. She went on about not seeing her father's Pierce Arrow. "I'm sure," she said, "Mother and Father didn't go away in it. Mother always complains that motoring is a dismal affair and she has to wrap herself in all sorts of scarves and put on a veil for protection against the dust and the wind. She'd much rather take the train, and Father admits that trains are a little more dependable."

Another time after hours and hours in that bed of hers, she said, "I don't understand why I'm tired all the time. Cora always says I have more stamina than any girl in school."

Goodness knows I'd wondered why that hadn't bothered her, and now that it finally did, I suppose I should have picked up on it. But I guess I just didn't have the courage to bring matters to a head on my own. One thing, she did seem to make an effort to eat more after that.

Before I knew it, it was Friday, nearing the end of my third week on The Hill. I almost forgot about Neena. If I was going to take her to Parker it would have to be tomorrow. That was what was on my mind when I looked out the front window about one o'clock and saw Buzz poking his way up the road toward the house and looking as though he'd lost his last friend.

Buzz is a happy-go-lucky kind of kid, and I wondered why he had such a long face. I shouted a greeting and hurried down the path to meet him.

14.

"Well, this is a surprise. What's on your mind, Buzz?"

"I sure miss you, Losie." Even his voice was sad. "You aren't home very much."

"I'm sorry." I didn't know whether I ought to tell him about this thing I was into. Would he really understand? But I did remind him that I was helping Dev out by staying with her mother who wasn't well.

"I know that," he said, "but are you gonna live up here forever?"

"Of course, not forever, Buzz. The summer's only started."

He squinted up at me and there was worry in his eyes. "Are you all right?"

"Sure I'm all right. That's a funny question. Why wouldn't I be?"

He sort of kicked at the dust and then carefully smoothed it out with the toe of his tennis shoe. He sure had something on his mind. "Because," he said, "well, because my friend Corky says Mrs. Skinner is a crazy old lady."

"Why, Buzz! I'm surprised you'd pay any attention to that kind of talk. And where, for heaven's sake, did Corky hear such a thing?"

"His dad delivers the mail out here. He told Corky he'd better stay away from this place."

"Well, you just tell Corky there is nothing for him, or you, to worry about. I told you Dev's mother isn't well right now. She's had trouble, Buzz. One day you'll understand that things happen to people sometimes when they have trouble."

"What kind of things?"

"Well, once in awhile they act differently, not like they used to. Besides you know I'm a scaredy cat. I wouldn't be up here if there was anything to be afraid of." Boy, I bit my tongue on that. In the beginning I hadn't felt too good about this myself.

Anyhow what I said seemed to make him feel better, and we went on to lighter subjects. We talked about his polliwogs and his pet rabbit, Licorice, and he told me Neena played double solitaire with him and was pretty good. "I beat her easy though," he said. "She was one-handed."

I rumpled his hair and promised to be home before long to give him some competition. Then a good thought came to me. "Say, I haven't had lunch yet, and I know you can always eat. How would you like to have a picnic? We could fix some sandwiches and there are bananas and cookies in the house. We could go down the hill a way and sit under the elm trees. Would you like that?"

"Sure. That'd be keen."

At the kitchen door Buzz hung back at first until I told him Mrs. Skinner was busy upstairs. I knew she was deep into *Madame Bovary*. She'd told me, in fact, just to let her alone for awhile.

I found a couple of decks of cards in a kitchen drawer and tucked them in the basket along with the food, and I also found an old blanket to spread out on the grass.

"We're in business," I said, but before we left the house I went up to see if Mrs. Skinner needed anything. She just waved me off. She wanted to finish her book.

"I'll be outdoors for awhile but within shouting distance," I said, not telling her I had company. "If you want me, just call."

Then Buzz and I meandered down the road until we found a likely spot.

"It was nice of you to come see me, Buzz. I do miss being at home, and I've got to call Neena tonight. She ought to be able to get that cast off tomorrow. I hope to take her to the doctor. Maybe you'd like to go along."

"She went today," said Buzz as though I should have known. "Dad took her."

"Oh." Darn it, being stuck here on The Hill had a lot of drawbacks.

"Dad told Mom he wanted to ask the doctor himself if Grandma's arm was all right. They'll be home tonight by suppertime."

I wondered what happened to Neena's private business, but Buzz wasn't the one to ask. I'd have to find out later.

It was fairly cool under the elm trees and, in spite of the ants and the grasshoppers, we had a good picnic. We'd pretty well wiped out the food and were into a hot game of double solitaire when there was a sound of shuffling along the road off to the side of us. Apparently Buzz didn't hear it, but I stopped playing and looked up. Mrs. Skinner stood in the shadow of the trees. She'd changed from the rose robe to a summer dress, one I hadn't seen before. It was a pale green dotted swiss that actually looked pretty good on her. But right then I didn't much care what she looked like. I was remembering how cross she'd been when "Annie" had had a visiting friend. Oh, boy, I thought, she's not going to like this, and sure enough she spoke in Mrs. Skinner's sharp voice. "Who is that boy?"

Well, I wasn't going to be ruffled. What could she do to me? Let her say whatever she wanted. I didn't even get up.

"This is my brother," I said, "Buzz. He just came to have lunch with me. I'll send him home though if you say so."

"Why?" The voice was Malvina's all of a sudden, and with almost a pleading in it, "I'd rather you asked me to join you."

She dropped down on the blanket, sitting cross-legged as though this was the natural position for her. She looked comfortable. I'd sure never seen my mother sit that way.

Buzz's eyes were as big as plates and his face went a little white. Quickly he moved away from her.

I don't think Malvina noticed. She arranged her skirt around her ankles and leaned toward him. "Double solitaire, hmm? I like card games," she said. "But I only get to play when Mother isn't around. She says there's a devil in every card. I don't believe that, do you? I know my father doesn't. He plays poker. Not with me, of course, because of Mother, but I learned by watching. We play cards a lot at school."

Our game had been interrupted and Buzz said, "Come on, Losie, let's finish. I can't do anymore until you find your five of diamonds." He kept a wary eye on Mrs. Skinner.

"Go ahead," she said. "Finish your game." And she sat quietly by until the last card was in place.

"There," said Buzz, "I won. I beat you three out of five, Losie. I'm the champion."

"But I haven't had my turn," said Malvina unexpectedly. "You can't be the champion of The Hill until every challenger has a chance. I'm good at double solitaire."

Buzz gave me a get-me-out-of-this look, but I didn't come to his rescue. "She's right," I said. "Separate the decks."

"I'll do part of them," said Malvina. As she reached toward Buzz her hand touched his. I saw him flinch a little, but he gave her half the pile.

How could anybody be frightened of those hands of hers— lovely, long slender fingers and nails buffed to a shine. And they were fast and sure as she sorted the cards.

Buzz was in a spot, but I figured it wouldn't hurt him.

"I'll watch this time," I said. "Let's see what happens."

Old Buzz likes a challenge and although he was chewing on his lower lip like crazy he spread his cards out and said he was ready.

Once the game started there was no stopping it, and I think when Buzz saw Malvina's fingers fly back and forth across the blanket he forgot about Corky.

They played four games, and Buzz won them all. He was feeling pretty pleased with himself, but Malvina said one day she'd teach him rummy, which took more than blind luck, and she'd show him a thing or two. She also said she was hungry and what had we had for our picnic. Buzz handed her the bas- ket, and she ate the one remaining peanut butter sandwich and a couple of cookies. The afternoon wasn't too bad.

Finally, Buzz said he'd better head on home. Mom would be wondering where he was. Malvina, and it was definitely Malvina the girl, told him to come back soon. "You know The Hill is a great place to play," she said. "There are a lot of trees to climb, and you might even build a house in one of them."

I squeezed Buzz's hand in a kind of secret code. *You see there's nothing to fear from Dev's mother.*

After Buzz scooted on down the hill I folded up the blanket. "You were nice to him," I said. "Thank you."

"I like your brother," she said, surprising me again by linking her arm in mine as we walked along toward the house. "I always wanted a brother."

"Oh," I said. "I have two, and it's a sister I'd like."

"Well, I didn't have a sister either, but Mother said I always leaned toward the boys." She winked and once more the sparkle was there in her eyes. What a knockout she must have been when she was really nineteen, with that lush red hair and creamy skin.

Together we went in through the front door. I thought the discussion was finished but she tossed her head and with a warm smile said, "Water under the bridge now—having a brother. One day I'll just have to get myself a son." She took her arm from mine and went up the stairs.

It wasn't until later that her words hit me. I had to hurry to get supper. Thank goodness there was some leftover roast. I made a stew, and while it simmered on the back burner those last words of Malvina simmered there too. Mrs. Skinner had wanted a son.

She didn't come down again, and there was nothing unusual about the upstairs supper service. It went according to schedule with little or no conversation.

Dev was late getting home and her mother was well settled for the night by the time we sat down to our own bowls of stew. I reported the day's happenings and even told Dev what her mother had said about a son. Perhaps I shouldn't have, but it seemed important. "Maybe the time is ripe," I said, "to come right out and say, 'Well, you didn't have a son, you know. You had a daughter—have a daughter. Don't you remember?' "

Dev said, "It's up to you, Lois. If you think that's what should be done." She seemed to have lost some of her interest in this whole thing, and I realized that her life had slipped into a different pattern. She was removed from her mother in a way—had become an outsider. I was the one in the middle. And was I now the one with the problem? That was a thought I tucked away in my mind. I wouldn't deal with it right away. I wasn't going to decide about talking to Mrs. Skinner either. Not yet.

Before it got too late I called to chat with Neena. Yes, the cast was off and she really could have gone back to her own house, but Dad wouldn't hear of it. She had to return to Bannister and finish out her visit. I asked about the private matter. Was she able to take care of it?

"Yes," she said.

I wasn't convinced. "With Dad around?"

"While your father was checking the lights and gas at my house, I used my neighbor's phone."

She might as well have said mind your own business. I knew the subject was closed.

I went to bed that night with all sorts of things in my mind. Buzz wanted me home. Neena could have used me. Dev was backing off. And all my efforts to put Mrs. Skinner and Malvina together again seemed to be at a standstill. I was discouraged.

But then on Saturday morning I found the letter.

15.

The letter. It was quite by accident that I found it. No, "found" isn't the right word. That makes it sound as though I was looking, and I didn't even know there was a letter.

To begin with, Saturday started with a difference. When I took the usual breakfast tray upstairs, Malvina—and more and more I was thinking of her as Malvina—asked if Buzz could come up again. I said not today. He had chores to do at home.

"Then maybe tomorrow," she said. "Sunday, before you leave for the afternoon."

I said if I had a chance I'd ask him. It was the first time she'd really planned ahead, giving a day and a time. I wondered if that was a good sign. And when I went back an hour later to take away the tray, I noticed she had eaten most of her breakfast. Was that good too?

About eleven she came downstairs, dressed in the dotted swiss again. She dawdled at the piano for awhile, seemed restless. Then to my surprise she settled into one of the leather chairs in the library.

"I didn't quite finish my book yesterday, Lois. I wonder if you'd bring it down to me. I think I'll read here. It's so pleasant."

"Sure," I said. "Is it on your night table?"

"Oh my, no. It's hidden away. In the bottom drawer of my dresser. I wouldn't think of leaving a book like that out in plain sight—not in my father's house."

Goodness knows I could understand that. It was only a couple of years ago I was caught up in *Anthony Adverse*. I was teaching in the country then and living at home. Believe me, I gave Anthony a brown paper jacket and threw him in with the third grade spelling books. Yes, I was with Malvina on this. I did say, however, that I hated to go poking around in her dresser.

"You won't need to poke," she said. "It's down on the left side just under the pile of winter nightgowns."

All the same I felt like a spy as I lifted out the flannel grannies and set them aside. The book was right where she said it would be, but underneath it there was something else which caught my eye—a small packet of mail. There was a rubber band around it, but it looked—what do I want to say?—*fresh*. I checked the top envelope. A telephone bill, and from the date I knew it was the missing one, the one Dev had expected three weeks ago. Okay, I might as well act the spy. I flipped through the rest of the stuff. The electric bill was there, too, along with a circular from the feed store. And then there was the letter.

The bills didn't matter anymore. Dev had called the utility offices long ago, asked for duplicates and paid them. The circular was a throwaway. Only the letter was worth pulling from the packet.

It was obviously good stationery and was addressed in a strong scholarly hand, a woman's I thought, to Mrs. Henry Skinner.

The return was imprinted on the back flap. Mrs. J.F. Collingsworth, 1612 Bayberry, Evanston, Illinois. It was sealed with one of those blobs of wax and stamped with the initial C. The seal had not been broken.

An unopened letter is always a little intriguing, and this one especially so. It might hold information that would be helpful, or even if it didn't, maybe when Dev's mother saw her name written out like this in what was probably a friend's hand it would do something for her. In spite of my gray mood of last night, I couldn't help being eager to find out, and after I put the nightgowns back in place I hurried down to the library and Malvina.

"Here's your book," I said, "but did you know there was mail in that drawer?" And without waiting for an answer, "One letter that was never opened."

"Oh," she said. Complete innocence. "Is it from Mother? Sometimes she writes long boring letters to me when she's away. I don't always read them."

"No," I said. "This is from a Mrs. Collingsworth." I held the envelope out to her.

She didn't take it and simply said, "I don't know anybody by that name."

I wasn't going to let it end there. I put the letter in her hands. I wanted her to see that it was addressed to her.

"Mrs. Henry Skinner?" she said without a flicker of recognition. Then she handed the envelope back to me. "This isn't even for me. Toss it out, Lois. Or maybe you should give it back to the postman. He's obviously delivered it to the wrong house."

I did neither of those things, of course, but I pressed it no further. I was getting used to disappointments like this. I slipped the letter into my pocket and when I went back to the kitchen I put it in the cupboard behind the sugar bowl. Tonight I'd give the thing to Dev, see what she had to say. I didn't feel as though I should open it, but she could.

The rest of the day I was kept very busy. Now that Malvina didn't stay in bed as much as she used to, there was more for me to do. Besides, I found myself volunteering for extra work. For instance, the business of that dotted swiss dress. In my mind I had figured out where the tucks could be deepened and how much the seams should be taken in so that the thing would fit her better. When I saw her pull the sash tight around her waist and look in the hall mirror, I said, "It's a little big, isn't it? You know I could alter it."

"That's a good idea," she said. Another surprise. "I don't know what Mother was thinking about to get a dress for me that was the wrong size. You can do it right now if you want."

You see how I got myself into that. She changed to another dress and turned the dotted swiss over to me on the spot. As she watched me work, she said, "I think I'll go down to Miss Harriet and see about a suit for school."

I thought she meant right then. Boy, wouldn't that be something if she struck out for town all by herself. But she said, "Still, if you can sew, Lois, I'd just as soon give the job to you."

Then later in the day I had the same worry all over again. It was long after lunch—which she ate in her room, and I mean *ate*. She came hurrying down the stairs and announced that she was going for a walk. Well, she'd taken walks before around the yard, but this time she started down the road at a fair pace. Believe me, I kept my fingers crossed. When she got out of my sight beyond the bend I really began to wonder what I'd do if she didn't come home. Maybe she *was* going to the dressmaker. I might have to go after her. Good thing I had Betsy.

In a few minutes, though, she came into view again on her way back. I was glad that she was getting stronger and had more vitality, but she was changing so. It had been simpler for me when she just stayed upstairs. I breathed easier when she said she was tired. It was no wonder. She'd had more exercise in the last two days than in all the time I'd been here.

I was tired myself, but I had the letter to look forward to. By six o'clock I was impatient for Dev to get home.

"Hurry," I said when Mr. Emmett let her out of the car. "There's something I have to tell you."

"Mama's back?" she said wearily.

"No. I should have said I have something to show you." I pulled her into the house and took the letter from the cupboard. We sat down together at the kitchen table. "Remember that Wednesday when there was no mail. Well, I found it—the bills—and this too." I handed her the envelope. "It must have come the same day. Your mother said she didn't know anyone by the name of Collingsworth. Do you?"

"Sure. That's her friend, Cora."

"Oh, I wish I'd known. Of course, Mrs. Collingsworth wouldn't mean anything to her. Cora wasn't married then. She was in school."

"I don't think they've seen each other since college. They tried to get together once or twice, but something always prevented it. I remember once it was because I got the measles. But they always kept in touch—long letters at Christmastime. Mama never shared them with me, but I knew she looked forward to getting them. I'm sure Mrs. Collingsworth wrote the last three Christmases too, but I have no idea whether Mama did."

I pointed to the envelope which Dev still held. "I hoped the name Henry Skinner would mean something to her. Didn't you say your dad dated your mother while she was in school?"

"Not until her sophomore year. They didn't even know each other when she was a freshman."

"Oh," I said, now feeling more like the detective than the spy. "That explains that. She hasn't met your father yet. Anyhow we can see if the letter gives us something to go on." Dev was turning the envelope over and over in her hands but made no move to break the seal, and I said, "You're going to open it, aren't you?"

"I've never opened her mail—never. It was something she wouldn't allow."

"That's being silly."

"It's not silly. You don't know Mama. You said you didn't."

"But Dev, we're not dealing with your mother now. We're dealing with someone who needs help. If Doctor Byford were here he'd tell you to open it. You know he would."

"I can't, Lois. I just can't."

"Then I will. This is one decision I'll make." I snatched the letter from her and tore it open. Dev turned away for a minute, but when I pulled out the folded notepaper she leaned toward me.

The greeting was in the same positive hand as on the envelope. *Dear Mookie,* Mookie! No one but a best friend could get away with using a nickname like that. The letter was short and I read it out loud.

No word from you for the last three Christmases. What goes on? There are only two answers I can think of. You are either mad at me—though I can't imagine why—or you're dead. Well, if you're dead, that's all right, but mad I won't accept. I have sent out the bloodhound, my son, Paul. He's been going to school in Arizona—the dry air is supposed to be good for him—and I've talked him into swinging up to Bannister on his way home to check on you. I hope my letter reaches you before he does, but no matter. He's a personable boy, like his father. You'll probably see him coming. He bought a car out there he tells me. A roadster— bright yellow.

That was all. Cora got right to the point and signed off. *Love. Cora.*

"The Mayor of Lodi," I sputtered. This time there could be no question about it.

Then I realized something else. This new discovery blew Truman McChesney right out of the picture.

16.

"But Dev," I said as soon as I put my thoughts together, "your mother told Mr. Erickson her caller was Truman McChesney."

Dev came right back at me, and she seemed a little annoyed. "Are you sure, though, that she was talking about that day, that particular day when she suddenly changed? I've explained to you that Mama hasn't had a solid hold on time for ever so long. Maybe this Truman did visit her. But when? It could have been anytime. She didn't tell me what she did while I was at work. She could have had a hundred callers in the last three years without my knowing it."

"You're probably right," I said, remembering Malvina's uncertainty with the minister. "I guess we can forget Truman. At least we know for sure now that the guy in the yellow roadster was Paul Collingsworth, and I know for a fact he was looking for your house on that Wednesday. If I could have sprung all this on your mother this morning, I wonder what she would have done."

"It isn't too late for you to find out. Go ahead. Talk to her if you think it will do any good."

There was that note of detachment again. I didn't like it, and I said, "Now that you're here, Dev, I think you should be the one to talk to her."

"But I'm Annie. Don't forget that. And Lois, I'm just too tired tonight to have her tell me again I don't belong in this house."

I couldn't blame her, but I did feel she should handle this. "Okay," I said, "not tonight if you're tired. But you'll be here tomorrow. While I'm gone give her the letter. Tell her it's hers, that she is Mrs. Henry Skinner, that Mrs. Collingsworth is her old friend, Cora, that they aren't schoolgirls anymore, they're grown women, and tell her you know Cora's son, Paul, was here to see her and you want to know what happened." I stopped for breath. "And while you're at it tell her Cora may have had a son, but she didn't. She had a daughter. Maybe it's time to do away with Annie."

"Just like that." Her words were heavy with sarcasm. "You make it sound so easy, Lois, so reasonable, but Mama is without reason." Dev looked down at her hands which were clasped tightly together, the knuckles white, and then she said, "Maybe that's the point. When Doctor Byford comes home I just ought to tell him he'll have to do something about her."

"Dev, you don't mean that."

"How do you know I don't?" Her voice had a sharp edge.

"But she's your mother."

"Mother? Oh, she laid down the rules to form my character, prodded me into getting good grades. Mama always had a sense of duty. Pride too. She gave me the best clothes and piano lessons. But she wanted a son all right. I could have told you that."

"I don't think that makes any difference now."

"Maybe to you it doesn't." We'd been sitting at the kitchen table all this time, and now Dev got up and moved around the room. "All my life," she said, "I've tried to please her. She didn't seem to notice anything I did. And in these last years, while I was holding our lives together, she just took what I had to give and returned nothing."

"It was awful for you, I know."

"You don't know. You couldn't possibly know what it's been like." Dev's voice lifted in something close to anger. "I know she had a breakdown, but for three years to barely talk to me? And mostly to complain? Now this business of being nineteen again and she throws me out into limbo. Then you came—and don't think I don't appreciate it—but do you realize I haven't even seen Mama in three weeks? And she hasn't asked for me? As far as she's concerned, there is no Devonnabelle Skinner. I look at things in a different light now. Why should I care!"

"But you've got to care, Dev. She needs you."

"No, she doesn't. She has you." There was the anger again and now it seemed to be pointed in my direction. "If you want to follow through on this letter thing, that's all right with me. She's more apt to respond to you anyhow." Dev stopped and looked at me with a kind of defiance. "At times I'd just as soon Mama wouldn't come back."

I don't think I'd ever seen Dev in a mood like this. It took me off guard. She was always such a mouse, never stood up to anybody. I could think of nothing more to say, and since she had apparently spoken her piece to the finish, a silence settled between us.

In an effort to busy myself I started dishing up our supper. I'd made macaroni and cheese during the afternoon. Malvina said she was hungry for it. She'd eaten early. I'd already brought down her empty tray. I didn't think we'd hear from her anymore for the rest of the evening. Dev set the table and the two of us moved carefully around each other.

I was still puzzled about her anger, and a new thought came to me. Did Dev resent the fact that I could get to her mother when she couldn't? It sure sounded that way. But no, I wouldn't believe it—not of Dev.

Do you know we sat through our meal without a word? Like a couple of strangers sharing a table at the bus station coffee shop. I started to say something once or twice but changed my mind. Dev was right. How could I ever understand what she'd been through?

I don't know what Dev was thinking about, but my thoughts were bouncing all over the place. Maybe I had become too involved. Shouldn't I be working on my own problem? We were three weeks into my summer. I'd been dipping into my savings to buy some of the food here at the Skinners. It was only fair. But I couldn't go on like this indefinitely. Maybe I was taking too much responsibility. Dev and I seemed almost to have changed places. And now there was this new attitude of hers. If Dev was willing to give up on her mother maybe that's the way it should be. Still, something had happened to me—inside. I couldn't bear the thought of Malvina being "put away." I had grown to like her. But I hadn't liked Mrs. Skinner. Where along the way had that sparkling girl been lost? Dev seemed not to have known a lighthearted mother. Did she change when Dev was born or was it a gradual thing which began way back when Malvina Cameron brought a young husband home to Bannister? A husband who was handsome and likable but didn't know how to handle money.

Dev's dad used to come to the high school games with her sometimes, especially basketball. They seemed to have so much fun together. I wondered whether now Dev ever faced the fact that her father was responsible at least for these last three miserable years. She'd never talked to me about what happened. Not ever. My mother used to ask how she felt about her father's suicide. But Dev and I didn't become close friends until after it was all over, and if she didn't want to bring it up, I sure didn't.

We cleared away the dishes, working side by side with the silence still hovering over us, a silence filled with tension. I turned on the radio in the sunroom—"Your Hit Parade." I hardly ever miss that. And I hauled out my manicure set and started working on my nails. Dev found a book and we sat there together as we usually did. She seemed to be reading, but I noticed she sometimes went ten minutes at a stretch without turning the page, and every once in a while I caught her looking off into space.

It was she who finally said something. "Look, Lois, I apologize. I had no business spouting off at you. You're the best friend anybody could have, and you're right on one point. She is my mother. I can't wipe away my obligation. Besides, it isn't fair to you."

"I'm not complaining," I said. "We will have to tell your mother about the letter, but we've already decided it can wait until tomorrow."

I wanted to tell her about altering the dress and the other things that went on during the day, but I thought it best to stay clear of the subject of Malvina, and we went back to our separate occupations.

The evening did pass, and we were about ready to go to bed when the doorbell rang.

"I'll get it," I said, making a dash for the front hall. It was late. I was sure Mrs. Skinner was asleep, and I didn't want her to wake up.

Whoever it was apparently was in a hurry because the bell kept on ringing. When I opened the door I don't need to tell you I was surprised to see Twyla Erickson standing there on the welcome mat. But it wasn't Goody-Two-Shoes or the cocky gal who "liked Gully Huxton." It was a scared kid who pushed into the hallway with a great sigh. She was a bit of a mess. Her dress was torn, her makeup—and she had plenty on—was smudged, and her hair was all mussed up.

"What in the world happened to you?" I asked, and Dev, who had come up behind me, gasped, "You've had an accident."

"Oh, Devonna," Twyla sobbed. Maybe she was ignoring me, but I wasn't surprised that it was Dev she went to. They're almost the same height, and I can't see anyone over five-foot-three falling onto my shoulder without feeling silly.

Dev pulled the poor girl into the living room and sat her down on the nearest sofa. "There," she said, pushing the limp strands of hair back off Twyla's forehead. "Go ahead and cry."

I thought we could do with less crying and said, "I suggest you tell us what happened."

Twyla burst into a fresh set of tears and sputtered, "It's Gully."

Dev found a handkerchief in her pocket to stem the flood. "You mean," she said, "you and Gully had an accident?"

I took in the tangled curls and the smeared lipstick and knew that wasn't what she meant at all. They'd been down under the elm trees. I was sure of it. Even if the rules about parking on The Hill hadn't changed, Gully'd think they didn't apply to him. Hadn't he dated the child of the castle?

Dev was still playing the comforting mother. "Calm down, honey," she said. "Tell us about it."

Twyla blotted her eyes with the handkerchief and then settled back on the couch. "Well," she said, "I've been seeing him— Gully—a lot the last two weeks, and he's been real nice. I generally meet him at my friend's out at the edge of town. I can't have him come to my house. My father thinks I'm out with . . ." She gave me a guilty look. ". . . with Harvey."

"That's interesting," I said. "Doesn't your father think it's funny that Harvey doesn't come to pick you up?"

"No. I just call Father from Edna's. I don't actually say I'm with Harvey—just that I'm going to The Hill." She dabbed at her eyes again. "He knows you're here, Lois, and he thinks if I'm coming here I must be with your brother. That's the way my father figures things out. I don't exactly lie. We do always end up on The Hill."

She looked down at her feet. Embarrassment. Twyla knew that I knew the score. That was probably Gully's car I saw the Sunday night I came back after my set-to with the folks. "Anyhow," she went on, and now it was as though she had to get the whole thing out in a hurry. "Tonight I think he'd been drinking a lot before he met me, and he didn't want to go to the dance in Redmond. He didn't want to go out to Johnnie's. He didn't even want to go for a ride. He just wanted to . . ."

"Park?" I said.

Her face got very red but she barged on. "He'd been telling me how he planned to buy a little business, maybe a grocery

124

store or a poolhall and that he was ready to settle down. He said that's what his folks wanted him to do, and he said he thought he'd found the girl to do it with. He hadn't talked like this before and it was kind of exciting. After all I am out of high school and have to think of my future. Anyhow we kissed a little and then he got awful fresh and I said I'd better go home."

"And, of course, he didn't offer to take you." I couldn't avoid the sarcasm.

"Gosh, no. He said I was acting like a child and why didn't I grow up. I opened the car door, but he pulled me back. That's when my dress got torn. And it's my best dress. Anyhow I finally got away from him and ran up here. I looked back once to see if he was following me, but he was just sitting on the running board with his head in his hands. I don't think he was feeling too good."

"We won't worry about Gully," said Dev. "What we need to do is get you looking presentable again. You can use the washroom off the front hall."

I could be just as practical. "If you'll give me your dress," I said, "I think I can stitch it up a little."

"Thanks," Twyla said, slipping the pongee sheath off over her head. She picked up her white straw purse from the couch, but before she left the room she turned to Dev. "Did Gully ever try to get fresh with you?"

Dev smiled. "No. I knew only the 'nice' Gully. And he could be charming. Remember, though, that was three years ago. We were both in high school. Besides, I didn't have many dates with him. It was in the spring, just before we graduated."

I knew Dev and I were having the same thought and I wanted to get rid of it. "Run along, Twyla," I said. "And for heaven's sake wash your face."

Dev got the sewing box for me, and I looked at the tear. It was just the seam—no big deal. I could fix it.

When Twyla came back she looked better. She put on her dress again and said, "Thanks. You've been real sweet."

The whole incident had taken only fifteen minutes or so. I was about to say I'd take Twyla home when there was a terrible banging at the door, and over the noise Gully was shouting at the top of his lungs. "Hey, in there. Open up!"

"Don't let him in," said Twyla, and she actually tried to hide behind me.

"I want my keys," yelled Gully.

"His keys?" I said. "Do you have his keys?"

She looked sheepish. "I thought if he couldn't drive the car he couldn't come after me."

"Well, that was dumb. You might know he'd have to come after you then. You'd hardly expect him to leave his car on The Hill and walk back to town. Anyhow let him in, for goodness sake. And let's keep our voices down. We don't want to disturb Mrs. Skinner."

Dev opened the door and Gully practically fell into the room. He may have had too much to drink, but now he was mostly mad. "Okay, Twerp," he said, "where are they?"

Twyla got the keys from her purse and threw them on the floor in front of him.

He bent unsteadily to pick them up, and when he straightened he took the three of us in with a bleary eye. Settling on Dev, he said, "Old home week, eh?"

"If you say so," said Dev gently. "We've changed, though, haven't we, Gully?"

It was one of those moments when no one has anything to

say. Then out of the quiet and from somewhere above us . . .

"Devonnabelle!"

We all looked to the staircase. There was no one to see. There was only the voice, which was coming through the open door of Mrs. Skinner's room. It was clear and commanding. "If that Huxton boy is down there, send him home. You're seeing too much of him. Devonnabelle! Do you hear me?"

17.

Oh, boy, how do you top that for drama! Of course, I'm sure it didn't mean anything to Gully. He'd probably been called on this carpet before. And I don't think Twyla got the picture at all. Only to Dev and me was there any real importance to the moment. As we looked at each other you could almost hear the questions rattling around in our heads, and then Dev called out, "Yes, Mama, I hear you. Gully's just leaving. Go back to sleep."

I felt a wave of relief. Dev was going along with it. For a few minutes I thought Mrs. Skinner might appear, but she didn't. Dev must have said the expected thing.

Gully did leave. I practically pushed him out the door. Not that he wasn't ready and eager. He didn't offer to take Twyla home, and I think he was afraid we'd insist. I wish we had. She was sort of on our hands, all the while just standing there look-ing as though she might cry again.

Earlier I'd been ready to drive her back to town. It would take me away from the house for a little bit. Now I hated to leave. I might miss something. Still, it had to be done.

"Come on, Twyla," I said. "I imagine you're anxious to get home. Let's go."

I don't think she was anxious at all, but I got her to the front door. Dev had followed along behind us and, trying to sound casual, I said, "You'll go up to see your mother, won't you?"

"I suppose so," she answered, but there wasn't much enthusiasm.

"Just do it." I gave her a hard look. There was a lot more I wanted to say but didn't think I should with Twyla there. All I could do was leave.

Betsy hadn't been driven for a couple of days, and it took me awhile to get her started. That was all right. In spite of the fact that I was in a hurry, I was glad to give Gully time to get away. I didn't want to see anymore of him.

There hadn't been a word from Twyla for some time. Now as we drove along she said, "Thanks for taking me home. I don't know what I'd have done."

"That's okay. I'm just glad you found out about Gully for yourself."

"Yeah." She sounded a little disappointed.

"I hate to tell you I told you so, Twyla, but I did. You're lucky you didn't get burned."

"But he could be so nice. And he's terribly good looking. I just wanted to have a good time."

She was exasperating. "Look, Twyla," I said, "You've been living in some kind of a dream world. There's one thing you've got to learn. You just don't go out with a guy who has a reputation, no matter how good looking he is. A girl has to put herself on one side of the fence or the other. You can't sit on the top and choose whatever appeals to you at the moment. If you get down on the wrong side, it's pretty hard to get back up again."

"You sound like my father." Mention of her father brought a troubled look to her face. "You won't . . ."

"No," I said, answering her question before she asked it. "I told you I don't carry tales. But I think it would be a good idea for you to tell your father what you've been doing."

"He'd kill me."

"That's a silly thing to say. Sure, he'll be mad, but I think he'd be proud of you for being honest. I don't know your father too well, Twyla, but my folks say he's a fine man. You think he's too strict. Okay. We don't always have to see eye to eye with our parents, but as long as we live at home, we have to go by the rules they set up."

Just listen to me, I thought. I'm throwing myself in the same bundle with her. Then I added, "After you're on your own you can do whatever you like. Go out with all the poolhall guys in town if you want to."

Twyla was quiet for a few minutes. Then, as though she'd made up her mind about something, she said, "Harvey's asked me for a date next Thursday night, to go to the movie."

"Are you going?" I didn't really care. I wasn't trying to plead Harve's case.

"I haven't told him I would yet, but I guess so. Harvey's all right, and he sure can play those drums."

I could have told her that even that skimpy praise from her would put Harve on stilts, but I didn't want to give her the satisfaction.

By this time we were back in town. I avoided Main Street, going around behind the creamery. There might not have been anybody to see us, but I didn't take the chance.

The Ericksons live on the same street as we do only a few blocks farther west, and as I drove past our house I noticed that the porch light was still on. Harve probably wasn't in yet. Boy, wouldn't he flip if he knew what had been happening. But he'd never get the story from me.

Seeing our house reminded me that I hadn't talked with anybody there all day. I'd have to check with the folks tomorrow, see how things were. I remembered that Malvina wanted Buzz to come up in the morning, but after tonight everything on The Hill might be different again.

When we got to the Ericksons I pulled up in front, but Twyla didn't seem to be in a hurry to get out.

"Do you have a key?" I asked.

"The door's never locked," she said. But she still sat there, and I realized there was something on her mind.

"Okay, Twyla, what is it?"

She played with the clasp of her purse, opening and closing it in a nervous kind of way as she spoke. "Mrs. Skinner said—well you heard her—that Devonna was seeing too much of Gully. It sounded as if she was talking about right now."

"What are you getting at?" I was anxious to be through with this. "Dev told you it was three years ago that she dated Gully and not much even then. Are you trying to say she was lying?"

"Oh, no—no," she said quickly. "It's just that—well, the night I went to The Hill with my father, he said Mrs. Skinner told him to come back when her parents were home. That didn't make any sense. Her parents don't live there."

"So? What's your point?"

"I guess what I'm trying to say is that Devonna's mother . . . She still isn't well, is she? She's mixed up."

I hated to admit it, but I knew that's what she was getting

at. "You're right," I said, "but we think now maybe Mrs. Skinner's going to be better."

"I hope so," said Twyla. "I like Devonna. It must be sad for her."

And I thought this girl had no feeling for anyone but herself. "She likes you too," I said, remembering Dev's gentle comforting. I felt very small, and I'm not talking about my height. It just goes to show you how much a person can be wrong about another person.

Twyla opened the car door and with a "Thanks again," walked slowly up to the house. I waited until she got to the porch. It was the least I could do. Then, making a U-turn, I stepped on the gas and headed back to The Hill. I was dying to find out where things stood.

It looked as though Mrs. Skinner was catching up with her life, that now she was at least up to the year Dev graduated from high school. Maybe she was going to be all right.

I pushed Betsy to her limit even up the rutted hill road and when the house came into view I could see that there was no light in the big front bedroom. In fact, as I came closer and finally around to the backyard, I was surprised that the only light at all seemed to be the little one over the back door.

When I went into the kitchen I had a strange feeling of defeat. The house was quiet. Dev wasn't there waiting for me. I hurried up the back stairs. The door to her room was ajar, but there was no light there either.

"Dev," I called softly, and when I got no answer I flipped the switch. She was in bed. Not asleep, just lying there on her back staring up at the ceiling.

"What happened?" I said.

"Nothing, nothing at all."

"What do you mean? You went up to see her, didn't you?"

She turned to the wall. "Oh, I went to her room all right."

"Well? Didn't you talk to her?"

"No. She was asleep."

"If you went upstairs right after Twyla and I left the house, she couldn't have been asleep very long."

"I'm not sure she'd ever been awake."

"But she called out to you."

"I don't think she knows she did that."

"Darn it, Dev, look at me. Something made her say what she did. Why didn't you wake her? That was too good a moment to lose. You should have . . ."

"I don't want to talk about it, Lois. Just go to bed."

That made me mad, mad at everybody who had anything to do with this night, and especially mad at Dev. Maybe she hadn't gone in to see her mother at all. But if she wouldn't talk about it there was nothing I could do until morning. I clumped back downstairs to my maid's room and crawled into the sack.

18.

Neena says that with a good night's sleep and oatmeal for breakfast, you can handle anything. Well, I had both by eight o'clock on Sunday morning. We'd see.

I fixed Mrs. Skinner's tray and took it up by way of the front stairs. Even if Dev was awake and out of bed, I didn't want to run into her—not right away. I wanted to see her mother first, wanted to find out about last night.

The door to the master bedroom was open as usual, but for a few minutes I just stood there gathering courage. Suppose Mrs. Skinner had filled in her life up to three years ago. That would put her in the days when I wasn't altogether welcome on The Hill. What would she say about my being here at this hour of the morning, to say nothing of serving her breakfast? Wouldn't she wonder where Dev was? Ask for her?

I sure wasn't going to get any answers out in the hall, and bracing myself, I went in.

She was up, dressed and standing by the window. When I said, "Good morning," she turned to me. I recognized the college smile. Actually I felt relieved. I was comfortable with Malvina.

"I was planning on coming downstairs for breakfast," she said. "You know the only reason I've been eating in my room is because Mother won't allow it when she's home."

I let that bit of information breeze right by me. First things first. I set the tray down on the little round table in the corner of the room and pulled up a chair for her. "You might as well eat it as long as it's here and hot." I was anxious to turn the conversation to last night and I had thought of a way to lead into it. "You look rested," I said. "Did you sleep well?"

"Fine," she said, "and I do feel good." Then as though it was an afterthought, "I did have a funny dream though."

"Oh?" I tried to hide my eagerness.

"Yes." She cocked her head to one side—remembering I suppose. "Cora and I were in this strange room with my father and a lot of other people. There were loud voices. Someone was crying and somebody else shouted, 'Give me the keys to the bank.' I looked up at my father, but it wasn't my father at all—a much younger man. There was something familiar about him, but I didn't know him, and even as I watched, his face changed again. It was your little brother."

"Buzz?"

She nodded. "Then my mother called from somewhere, a second floor I think. 'Send that boy home,' she said." Malvina stopped talking and frowned. "That part was so real."

You better believe it, I thought.

"After that, everything shifted. You know how dreams are. All at once I seemed to be upstairs, sitting up in my bed. There was still a girl down there with Cora, but I couldn't see her face. She shouted up to me, 'Go back to sleep.' That was it."

Dev had been right. Her mother wasn't awake last night, and she must have called out from her bed. Then, mostly because I wanted to keep the conversation going, I said, "I don't think I have dreams. Or maybe I just forget them as soon as I open my eyes."

She had stayed at the window while she talked, but now she settled herself at the table and spread the napkin over her knees. "I don't dream often," she said, "but last night it was very vivid."

The dream had undoubtedly been triggered by what she'd heard while Gully and Twyla were there. I wondered if there was any way to get her to see the connection to reality. I sure wouldn't know how to go about it. One thing for certain she was Malvina Cameron this morning, more Malvina than ever. She had on the dotted swiss again which, of course, fit her now. There was color in her cheeks and even though her hairstyle was out of date it was attractive. She looked kind of young.

I suddenly realized I was staring at her. Quickly I moved the subject back to a safe point. "It's my afternoon off," I said, "but I'll fix your dinner first. You can come downstairs to eat that if you want."

"It is Sunday. I'd forgotten." She seemed disappointed. "But you were going to ask your brother if he'd come up and play cards with me again. Remember that. If it isn't convenient this morning, why don't you leave early and bring him back with you when you come. Don't worry about dinner. I'll fix something for myself."

That could be a problem, but for now I agreed. "At any rate," I said as I backed out of the room, "I'll see you before I go."

Dev was in the kitchen when I got downstairs, and I told her what I'd learned and that we were right back where we'd started.

Well, almost. "Your mother's been eating regularly and getting some exercise," I said. "She looks good."

"How do you mean 'good'?"

The question reminded me that Dev hadn't been with her mother since I'd come to The Hill. I tried to give her a picture and wound up by saying, "The main thing is she has more pep. She's going to be all over the house today. You might as well be prepared."

"Why don't I just leave with you?"

"And let her stay here by herself?"

"Yes. If, as you say, she has more vitality, she'll be all right."

"Then you don't intend to talk to her about the letter?"

"What's the use?"

I felt the same coolness from Dev that I'd felt last night. Again the responsibility seemed to be settling on my shoulders. I actually had the fleeting thought I should let Dev take Betsy for the afternoon and tell Malvina I'd stay with her. I shook off that idea before I acted on it.

"I think you're wrong not to talk to her," I said, "but okay. And if you want to go with me that's up to you."

"That's right. She is my mother."

I couldn't argue with that. I did say, though, that I thought we ought to have something ready for her to eat. I'd feel better if she didn't try to use the stove.

"I wouldn't worry about that either. Mama won't do crazy things. She may have forgotten who she is, but she wouldn't forget to turn off the gas. And in case you're wondering if they had gas when she was nineteen, they did. Grandfather Cameron always had the latest thing."

"Just the same this stove would be a lot different from the

one she'd expect to be using. Besides, she doesn't need a hot meal. It's going to be a scorching day. We'll make something picnic style."

That agreed on, we spent the next hour or so fixing potato salad and slicing up some cold ham and tomatoes. I did make a boiled custard and opened a package of Fig Newtons. All the time a persistent thought pecked at my mind. With Malvina's new energy, the chances were she would no longer be content to spend her evenings in her room and go to bed early. And if she was going to meander around the house, she was bound to run into Dev sooner or later.

It turned out to be sooner. Just a little after eleven she came into the kitchen, tray in hand, and found us clearing up our dishes.

She took one look at Dev and said, "Annie, what are you doing here?"

I could see Dev's throat muscles tighten, and I said, "You know she's my friend." I was going to say more but Dev spoke up and took another tack.

"I am not Annie," she said. "I've told you that. Besides, I am sick of this whole thing. You tell her, Lois. You make her understand."

Malvina turned to me with a question. "Make me understand what?"

It had certainly been dumped in my lap. This was not the way I wanted it, but what could I do?

"First of all," I started, "you're clear on one thing. You know I'm Lois."

"Of course, and you've said you're a friend of Annie."

"That's where it's wrong. There is no Annie here. I'm a friend of Devonnabelle Skinner and Devonnabelle is your . . ." I saw the blank look on her face. No, I wouldn't get anywhere going down that path. I backed up a little and came at it from another direction. "Why don't you sit down?" I said, and when she was settled on one of the straight kitchen chairs, I went on. "You remember that letter I gave you yesterday, the one I found in your drawer?" I didn't wait for an answer. "Well, it was—is— your letter. You are Mrs. Henry Skinner. That's what it is you have to understand."

The meaning of my words was completely lost on her.

"What kind of nonsense are you talking, Lois?"

"It isn't nonsense. You are Malvina Cameron Skinner now. Mrs. Skinner. And you have a daughter, Devonnabelle." I held my hand out toward Dev. "Here. This is your daughter. Please try to remember."

"Lois." There was annoyance in her voice. "Is this some kind of a game?"

"No game. That letter was from Cora. You do remember Cora. You tell me about her. She's an old friend and she is now Mrs. Collingsworth—has been for years. She wrote because she was worried about you, and she . . ."

Malvina stood up as though to end the conversation. "Now I know this is some kind of a joke. But I don't find it funny. I didn't expect this kind of thing from you, Lois. We've gotten along so well. I considered you almost a friend."

Dev just stood there, gave me no support. When I looked at her she spread her hands in a way that said plainly, "I told you it was no use. You might as well give up."

And Malvina Cameron simply turned on her heel and left the room.

I had to admit I'd accomplished nothing.

When we were ready to leave the house, I told Dev we ought

to check with her mother, and I found her in the living room sitting in one of the velvet chairs. She was very still and seemed to be staring out into the front yard.

I had no intention of trying to pick up the talk where we'd left it. I only said, "We're going now. I set out some food for you. You'll see. I won't be late."

She said nothing in reply.

A few minutes later we brought the car around from the back and were all set to head down the hill, when Dev said, "Look."

Mrs. Skinner was standing on the front porch watching us. I realized that although she'd seen Betsy in the yard she must be surprised to see me behind the wheel and driving away. Well, she was bound to see—really see—other surprising things today. Things she hadn't noticed before. Physically, she was stronger now, more alert, and she'd have the whole house to herself. I had the feeling she'd investigate the kitchen, the sunroom. There would be the stove, even if she didn't have to cook on it, the electric icebox, the radio and whatever else that couldn't have been there in 1913. Poor Malvina. Again I had the urge to stay with her.

"Do you really think," I said to Dev, "that she'll be all right?"

"Of course, she will." Dev was positive. "Besides, if she's going to stay this way, I'll have to begin leaving her alone sometimes. And we won't be away that long."

"Okay," I said. "I won't worry about it." But I didn't feel at all sure.

Dev leaned back against the car seat and heaved a big sigh. "Lois," she said, "do you realize we have the whole afternoon together and out of that house?" There was a kind of joy in her voice. "I'd like to have a good time."

19.

Once away from The Hill, the air seemed to clear between Dev and me. I could see now why she was discouraged, almost ready to give up on her mother. And as far as leaving her by herself for the afternoon, I guess I could understand the reasoning there, too, when I thought it over. Even though Doctor Byford had told Dev he didn't think Mrs. Skinner should be left alone, he probably didn't expect someone to be with her every minute. Anyhow, it was true we wouldn't be away long, and we sure could use some fun.

The arguments sounded good and I'd said I wouldn't worry, but I was still trying to convince myself as I said, "Okay, what do you want to do?"

"Promise you won't laugh."

"I wouldn't think of it," I said, feeling the old warmth of our friendship.

"Well, one of the Petersen girls came in the store yesterday and said there was a carnival over at Winona this weekend. It's been a long time since I've been on a merry-go-round. I'd like to go."

It troubled me a little that we'd not only be away from the house but out of town, but I said if it was what she wanted to do it was all right with me. "We'll just swing around by the church first. It should be letting out about now. I'll catch Mom and tell her not to count on me for dinner."

"Oh, Lois, I forgot that you usually go home. I don't want to interfere with your plans."

"You're not," I said. "I'd just as soon skip it today anyhow. We can drop by the house on the way back just to say hello."

I was right about the timing at the church. We pulled up in front just as the congregation began drifting out. The Reverend Mr. Erickson and his wife had taken a stand by the door and were shaking hands and chatting with the people who filed by. Twyla was beside them, starched and prim. She was smiling too, and when she saw us she waved. Everything must have turned out all right with her father.

I spotted Mom and Neena but couldn't get their attention. It didn't matter because Buzz came bounding over the churchyard to greet us.

"Are you coming home, Losie? Can I ride with you?"

"Gee, Buzz," I said. "I'm not going to be there today."

His face fell, but before I could say anything more, Dev told him where we were going and said, "Maybe you can come along."

That invitation didn't need repeating. "Oh, boy!" He looked at me. "Can I?"

"It's all right with me. Go tell Mom not to plan on either of us for dinner."

Buzz was off in a flash, and I called after him, "Tell her we won't be late."

I was glad to see Neena did have her arm out of the cast. In fact, I noticed it was with that right hand that she dipped into her pocketbook. She was giving Buzz money, of course. That was nice of her and I appreciated it. I would have treated him, but I was trying to go as easy as possible on my savings until I knew what was ahead.

Mom signaled her approval and sent Buzz back to us with the reminder to stop by the house for him to change out of his Sunday clothes.

That took only a few minutes and when he climbed into the rumble seat again we were off.

Winona is about the same size as Bannister, but I don't think it's as nice a town. Not quite as many trees and the stores on the main street aren't very interesting. There's no Ryan's, that's for sure. They do have this elm-shaded area out at the south edge of town though, and it's perfect for tent shows.

We had to park a little way from the grounds, and it was blistering hot, worse than it usually is in June—one of those days with no air stirring. As we poked our way across the dry grass, Buzz said, "Neena gave me a whole dollar. What shall I ride on first? The ferris wheel? And do I have to stay with you?"

"For heavens sake, no. Just run along, but remember, before you spend all your food money on cotton candy and ice cream, have a couple of hot dogs, maybe an ear of corn. Okay? I don't want to take you back to Mom with a stomachache. We'll meet you at the car at five."

"Five-thirty's soon enough," said Dev. "We got a late start. It's already after two."

I guess it was for her to decide and I said, "Five-thirty then. You can ask someone for the time."

He agreed and as he hurried on his way to the ferris wheel,

Dev shouted after him. "Hang on tight now. And don't look down."

Buzz taken care of, we were ready to map out our own afternoon. I love a carnival. I always thought it was so exciting that while everybody else in town is asleep the trucks move in and a whole different world is put together—a world with its own special sights and sounds. Smells too. Today it was the hot buttered popcorn that got to us first, and we shared a bag while we looked around to see what was offered.

Besides the ferris wheel there were several other rides for the kids. A merry-go-round, some of those little drive-it-yourself cars and a few live ponies—Shetlands. There were the skill games, too. A shooting gallery, darts, a penny pitch. The barkers, who all seemed to be wearing striped pants and colored shirts, tipped their straw hats to the crowd and invited everyone to win a prize.

Out in front of the sideshow the sword swallower was giving a sample performance. The more spectacular stuff was kept under cover. Folks had to pay to see the freaks. That certainly wasn't for me. Nobody should have to make a living that way.

One tent had flashy orange posters of dancing ladies. After sundown there'd be a girlie show.

The food concessions seemed to be bunched together, and Dev and I decided we were hungry when we saw those fat franks sputtering on the grill. The popcorn had made us thirsty too, and along with the hot dogs we bought strawberry pop and found a bench under the elms.

It promised to be a good afternoon, but I couldn't put Mrs. Skinner out of my mind. "Dev," I said, "I don't think we should stay until five-thirty."

"We just got here," she said, "and we'll be home long before dark. Nothing's going to happen to Mama."

Again I gave in, and while we ate we talked. During our evenings on The Hill, I had purposely avoided discussing my money troubles. The business with her mother was problem enough. I realized now that Dev didn't know anything about my plans for school and what had happened to them. When I told her she was a little upset.

"I feel guilty," she said. "If you hadn't come to help me you could have been out hunting for another job. All the more reason for my making some other arrangement for Mama. I've just got to."

"Hey," I said. "I'm not giving up my plans. They're just delayed."

"At least you have plans." She sounded depressed. "For three years I haven't been able to look beyond just getting along."

"You'd always planned to go on to school, Dev. Would you still like to? You were the one who always got the best grades."

"I don't really care anymore. I think I'd just like to have a home of my own and a family. More than just one child, though, I can tell you that." Suddenly she laughed. "But for a home and children you do have to have a man, and where would I get a man in Bannister? Come on," she said with a toss of her head. "How about the merry-go-round?"

"Sure," I said. And off we went to line up with the kids for tickets. When we climbed onto a couple of palominos, we saw that the only other riders over twelve were the moms and dads and the grandparents holding their little ones, but Dev said, "So what." We even changed horses and rode again. There's something about calliope music that lifts the spirit. Today, though, it didn't do much for me. As a matter of fact, an afternoon at a carnival should just whizz by, but I kept looking at my watch thinking it ought to be five-thirty. After the merry-go-round we had some ice cream and then Dev threw a few balls at the milk bottles and won a stuffed dog. It struck me that she was having a far better time than I was.

We didn't see much of Buzz—spotted him twice high on the ferris wheel and once on the merry-go-round. He always had something in his hands to eat. I guess his money was holding out. Then sometime in midafternoon we found him waiting to buy a ticket to the side show, and I realized I should have given him another instruction.

"Hold it," I said, pulling him out of the line. "You're not going in there."

"Why not? I just want to see the two-headed boy."

"No you don't. How would you feel if people came to stare at you?"

"I wouldn't care if they paid. Anyhow I only got one head."

"Never mind," I said. "You can find something better to spend your money on."

He grumbled but came away with us, and before long he was back on the ferris wheel.

We'd seen only a few people from Bannister, the Gundersons, Mr. Taylor with his grandkids, and Chuck Kline with a gang of friends. I didn't ask, but I wondered why Harve wasn't with them. Then about five we ran into the Ryans.

"Hello there," said Mr. Ryan. "We just got here. Is it worth the trip? Mrs. Ryan can't wait to see if there's a fortune teller."

"I don't know that there is," I said. "If so we missed her. But one thing, your wife had better keep you away from the dancing girls."

Mrs. Ryan's eyes twinkled. "I don't believe I can do that, Lois. Why do you think he came? But I'll hang onto him."

Mr. Ryan laughed, then turned to Dev. "By the way," he said, "how's your mother, Devonna? She wasn't well a couple of weeks or so ago." As he spoke he gave me a pointed look which told me he wouldn't let on that he knew Mrs. Skinner's real trouble.

Mrs. Ryan clucked her tongue at her husband. "Now, Tom, you know Devonna wouldn't be here if her mother was sick."

Dev mumbled something about Mama being better, but I think Mrs. Ryan's remark hit home. A few minutes later when I said I'd seen enough and was ready to leave, she didn't put up an argument.

It took a little while to find Buzz, but as soon as we did we headed for the highway. On the way back we were quiet. Buzz, I'm sure, had plenty to say, mostly complaints about having to leave when he still had a dime left, but back there in the rumble seat he couldn't have made us hear him if he tried.

Anybody could guess what was on my mind, and Dev must have been having the same thoughts. She finally said, "Lois, maybe we should go right to my house. We can get Buzz home later."

"Your mother wanted to see him again anyhow," I said, and drove a little faster. It was still daylight when we got back although it had clouded over and the sky was hazy. I couldn't help thinking that almost every time I had driven to the Skinner house lately I found something unexpected. Tonight we were halfway up the hill when we heard the music, and when we reached the backyard Paul Whiteman's orchestra blared at us through the open windows.

Dev and I exchanged looks and got out of the car as quickly as we could. I said, "Wait here," to Buzz and then followed

Dev through the kitchen. The refrigerator stood wide open. All the cupboard doors were ajar. And in the sunroom the radio was going full blast. Mrs. Skinner was sitting in one of the wicker chairs, her hands folded in her lap, and she was crying.

Dev went right to her mother. "Mama," she said. "Are you all right?"

No answer. I turned the music off but stayed in the background.

"Mama," Dev said again, dropping to her knees and taking her mother's hands in her own. "Were you frightened? Do you want to tell me about it?" Then with unbelievable and unexpected gentleness, "It's all right. I'm here now." To me she said, "I don't think she even hears me, but at least she isn't pushing me away. If I'm still Annie she doesn't seem to mind. I'll see that she gets to bed and sit with her. You can run Buzz home."

"Fine," I said, feeling almost like an intruder. As I turned to go I heard Dev say in a crooning voice, "There, there, Mama, don't cry."

20.

For the second night in a row I was driving away from a dramatic moment just to take somebody home. But tonight I was glad to be leaving.

Buzz stayed in the rumble seat. I didn't explain anything to him. I had actually forgotten to tell him Mrs. Skinner wanted to see him again, and it wasn't important now. When we got home he jumped down onto the ground and ran to the house without any questions.

I closed the rumble seat and went up the walk. I wouldn't stay long, just wanted to say "Hi" to everybody. The way the vines grow around the front of our house you can't see onto the porch until you get there, and even though I heard Buzz talking to someone in his company voice I had no idea who it was. I certainly wouldn't have guessed it was Ben Oldham sitting in the porch swing with Neena.

"You never know when I'm going to turn up," he said, getting to his feet. "Hope you don't mind."

"What if I did?" I said with a laugh. "Would it do me any good?"

Neena reached over and patted Ben's arm. "If he'd come a little earlier," she said, "I'd have sent him over to Winona, but I was afraid you'd just pass each other on the road. So I kept him to myself. It isn't often I have the company of a nice young man."

"Where are the folks?" I asked.

It was Ben who answered. "Oh, they're here. I've been visiting with them too. They just went inside—to listen to Jack Benny I think. I haven't been here long and your grandmother has been taking good care of me, even fed me her special chocolate cake."

Neena beamed. "And I've been hearing all about Ben's farm."

"Well, not altogether mine yet," he said quickly. "Dad will keep working with me through the harvest, but the folks are definitely moving into town. It's all settled."

"That's great," I said. "Your future's all cut out for you. Wish mine was."

Neena got up and offered Ben her hand. "Now that Lois is here, I'm afraid I'll have to give you up. But you can come and visit with me anytime." Then to Buzz, who had been standing around listening, "Come on, Buzzie, tell me about the carnival."

After they went in the house, Ben and I took over the swing. I was a little uncomfortable, sticky and hot. I know my nose was shiny and I hadn't even bothered to put on any lipstick. Men do make me so mad sometimes. Imagine dropping in on me like this without warning. Oh, well, there wasn't anything I could do about it now.

Ben was full of talk. "That grandmother of yours is a sharp little lady. She's been briefing me on everything from Babe Ruth's batting average to the wiles of Wally Simpson, with a detour through politics."

"I'm not surprised. The world won't ever leave Neena behind."

"She also told me you're still staying with your friend. How soon do you have to get back there?"

"No hurry." I realized that Ben didn't know anything that had happened at the Skinners during the last three weeks, and I told him the whole story right up to tonight.

"The problem's still there then," he said. "Dev's mother living in another time."

"Yeah, and I sure wish something could be done about it. At least, though, she wasn't tossing her daughter out of the house tonight. It looks as if things may be back in Dev's hands again."

We let the subject drop there, and Ben asked if I would like to go for a ride. "It might be a little cooler out in the country."

"Sure," I said. "Just give me a few minutes to wash off the carnival grime. Go on in and join the family if you want. I won't be long."

"No need to interrupt their program," he said. "I'd just as soon wait out here."

The folks were glued to the radio all right, but I waved hello before I went upstairs. I did one other thing—called Dev to see if she needed me.

"No," she said. "Mama's in bed now. I couldn't get her to talk, but my guess is that many things around the house confused her, and when she finally flipped the switch on the radio and got music, especially at the volume she gave it, it was just too much. Poor Mama. I feel sorry for her. I've never seen her so helpless, so lost. She actually seemed to need me, want me to be with her. Anyhow she's quiet now—stopped crying."

"That's good," I said. Then I told her Ben was with me and as long as there was nothing I could do, I'd see her later.

I was glad she was taking charge again, and after I fixed my face, put on a fresh dress, and changed into my white sandals, I went back to Ben. We were heading for the car when we saw Harve running up the street toward the house. Harve doesn't usually move fast, and I could see he was pleased about something.

"Hey," I said, "what's the rush?"

"Gotta date with Twyla," he said breathlessly. "If I can get Dad's car."

Ben shot a questioning look at me. Of course, he didn't know the Twyla story either, but I'd cover that another time. For now I just said, "Harve's the envy of all the guys, Ben. Twyla's about the prettiest girl in town."

Harve sort of puffed up and then he said, "She thinks you're okay too, Lois. When did you make such a big hit with her?"

I avoided answering that. Instead I had another surge of good will. "Look, Harve, Ben can drop me off at the Skinners before he leaves for Spring Willow. Why don't you take Betsy? You can bring her back to me tomorrow sometime. No hurry."

He was elated. Betsy is much sportier than the old Dodger. When I gave him the keys, this time without all the do's and don'ts, he showered me with thanks. Hmm. Put a girl in Harve's life and you've got a nice guy. I felt good about him as Ben and I drove away.

Going for a ride is sometimes the only thing there is to do on a Sunday night. There's no dancing, except in the roadhouses like Johnnie's, and in the summer with the smoke and the heat and the crowded postage-stamp floor, you might as well be in a steam box.

Ben took to the graveled highway, and as twilight gave up to darkness we rode through the countryside wishing it would rain and knowing that even rain wouldn't cool us off. We'd be wet for a little while and then be worse off than before.

As I said, Ben was full of talk. He had such plans for the farm. "You know, Lois," he said, "one of the things I'm going to do is to plant more clover and alfalfa. They're drought-resistant crops. One of the men at school preached soil building until it came out our ears, and he was so right."

We drove all the way to Centerville. The coffee shop in the bus station there was still open and we stopped for some ice cream.

I didn't really feel like discussing me, but by the time we were back in the car and heading home, we got around to it. I told him I wouldn't be going to school in the fall—and why—and then we moved on to Mrs. Skinner and Dev again. "My staying there naturally can't go on forever either," I said. "I'm going to have to find some kind of a job. I've got to do something."

"You can marry me." Ben's words just rolled off his tongue like half-set Jell-O. He didn't even look at me.

Honestly, I thought he was joking, and I said with a little laugh, "Why, Ben Oldham are you proposing?"

We had just passed the Petersen place and were on that empty stretch of road that leads to The Hill. He pulled over to the side and turned off the motor. "Sounds that way." Then he did look at me, and I knew he was dead serious.

As for me, I was speechless.

"I didn't have too much to offer before," he said, "and besides you were more interested in black gold than a diamond. It's really what I had on my mind tonight, why I came to see you. The farm's practically mine now, and since you tell me your school plans aren't working out, how about it?"

I certainly hadn't expected this. What could I say?

"Golly, Ben," I stammered, "you know I like you a lot. But I don't think I'm ready. I'm not even sure I want to get married at all. I'm not giving up on school."

"Well, I won't give up either. Maybe I can break down your resistance. You know that geology business is going to be a long haul. Even with the few credits you'll be able to carry over from teacher's college, it'll probably take at least three-and-a-half years."

"I know that. I don't care."

He leaned over, took my face in his hands and kissed me. It was a slow, warm kiss, but tonight my feelings were all mixed up, and I guess I didn't give him the response he wanted there either. He straightened up behind the wheel and drove on. Was he mad? Or worse yet, hurt? I couldn't tell.

We zoomed up to The Hill and into the Skinners' driveway, going faster than I thought was smart. Before he turned off the lights of the car they focused for a minute on the front porch. The bright beam picked up Dev in her white dimity nightgown. She grabbed for her robe and slipped into it.

Ben got out of the car and opened the door for me. "I'll just run along," he said.

"But you can't." I needed to do something to give the evening a better ending. "I've told you so much about Dev. You've got to meet her."

"I don't think she'd appreciate us coming unexpectedly like this," he protested, but I said it didn't matter and pulled him along with me up the stone steps. He'd forgotten he'd come to see me without any advance notice.

I've always said Ben was easy to know and comfortable to be with. I'm sure Dev was embarrassed not to be dressed. Remember she didn't grow up with brothers. But after a quick introduction the three of us sat there together on the porch as though we'd done this every night of our lives.

We listened to the crickets and talked about the carnival and the heat. I know Ben stayed longer than he intended. When he did get up to leave, he said—and it was to both of us—"Next time I come maybe we can take in a dance around here. I promise to give you time to get ready." He hadn't said he'd find another fellow for Dev, but the thought flashed through my mind that it would never bother Ben to have a girl on each arm.

As he went to his car, he said something else. "I'm sorry about your mother, Dev. I hope it all works out."

I was afraid Dev would be upset that Ben knew about her mother, and when we were alone, I said, "I'm sorry. I had to tell him—to explain why I was living here."

But she wasn't upset at all. "It doesn't matter anymore," she said. "I called Doctor Byford tonight. He's coming back, leaving first thing in the morning."

21.

Dev and I weren't in any hurry to get to bed that night. The temperature had been up to a hundred during the day, and it was still miserably hot. That's one thing about a Nebraska summer. It doesn't cool off when the sun goes down.

We sat out on the porch for a long time. Dev didn't say what she'd told the doctor and I didn't ask. It was enough to know he was coming back. I didn't tell her about Ben's proposal either. I could see she liked him. In fact, she said, "Your Ben's a great guy." She'd probably say I was crazy to turn him down. We did talk about his promise to come back, though, and about other things, including the weather. When we finally went indoors it was from the frying pan into the fire. I don't perspire much, and the heat seems to build up inside me until I think I'll explode. I lay in bed without even a sheet over me and promised I would never complain next winter when the temperature drops below zero. As soon as it was light, I got up and took a cold shower.

Dev came down to the kitchen about seven. Her night hadn't

been any better, and I said, "I wonder how your mother got along."

"All right, I guess. I looked in on her a few minutes ago. She seemed to be sleeping."

An hour or so later, after we'd had something to eat, Dev said she'd take up a tray. "I'm anxious to know where I stand. I felt closer to my mother last night than I can ever remember, but I wonder how it will be this morning. I wonder who I am."

We sure were playing the guessing game a lot lately. Would Mrs. Skinner be nineteen or forty-two? Would she be cross or sugar sweet? Would Dev be her daughter or the hired girl? I was holding the thought that yesterday's shock might have put an end to the whole problem.

It hadn't though. When Dev came back it was with a mixed bag of news.

"I guess I'm still Annie," she said, "but Mama didn't question my being here. I think she was half asleep. She didn't say much at all. Never mentioned last night. Nor did I. I thought it would be better to let well enough alone."

The bad news was that her mother seemed to have a cold, and I said I was sorry. "A summer cold is such an awful thing."

"I hope that's all it is. Anyhow I'm sure she'll just want to stay in bed today."

Mr. Emmett's truck swung into the driveway then and Dev had to go. "I hate to leave you with this added responsibility, Lois. Doctor Byford should be home by late afternoon, and I'll see if I can get away early."

"Come on," I said, "I can handle things." In a way it was easier for me to have Mrs. Skinner upstairs. I wouldn't even go to her just yet. Give her time to eat her breakfast and me time for some thinking.

I was glad the doctor would be home before the day was over, especially now that Mrs. Skinner had this cold. Of course, Dev had called him because of yesterday's upset, and I was afraid to think what she expected of him. Darn it, I still felt that if we could only bridge those years, the years that stretched from school days with Cora to . . . Wait a minute. Cora. I don't know why I hadn't thought of it before. Cora Collingsworth might be the answer, the link between Mrs. Skinner's two worlds. If she is really the close friend she seems to be from her letter, maybe she'd come. It sounded as though she could afford it and time and distance don't change a person's deep down feelings. Of course, I'd have to ask Dev, and I called her at the store as soon as I knew she'd be there.

"Lois," she said, "you're a dreamer."

"It's worth a chance. The point is would you care if I called her? I'll pay for it."

"Go ahead if you want, but no matter who pays for it I think it's money wasted."

I didn't need her enthusiasm, only her permission. I remembered Collingsworth's street in Evanston—Bayberry—and I got ahold of Marcie who handles the switchboard in town, told her to place the long distance call.

My mistake was in not thinking out ahead of time exactly what I was going to say. When I heard a crisp "Hello" on the other end of the line and Marcie answering that she had a call for Collingsworth from Bannister, Nebraska, I couldn't get my thoughts together.

"Hello," said the voice again, eager now, "Who's calling? Mookie, is that you?"

"No," I groped for the right words, "but I'm calling for her—

that is, I'm calling about her. I—I met your son and . . ." I don't know why I said that.

"Paul isn't here," said the voice. "Actually we didn't see much of him. He got restless after a week or so—said he'd promised to stay awhile with a fraternity brother in Omaha, and then I think he had half a dozen other stops to make before heading back to Tucson. Are you the daughter?"

"No, I'm just her friend. Lois, Lois Appleby." I was messing it all up. "I've been staying with them, with the Skinners and . . ."

She was patient, I'll say that, and somehow in the next few minutes I must have made sense because she seemed to get the drift of what I was talking about.

"Yes, yes," she said. "I was upset when Paul told me about his stop out there. I was going to write again to ask what was wrong. Mookie—Mrs. Skinner—is very dear to me, even if we haven't been able to get together over the years." She waited for a moment as if expecting me to say something. When I didn't she went on, almost as though she read my mind. "You'd like me to come, wouldn't you? Yes, and perhaps I can. I'll see. I'll let you know. I do appreciate your call." Then in a flip tone which reminded me of her letter, she added, "And you tell Mookie she has no business going back to Lindenwood without me."

How about that!

She hadn't made it necessary for me to say much more, and when I came away from the phone I wanted to dash right upstairs and tell Mrs. Skinner that her friend might be coming to see her. But, of course, I couldn't. "Perhaps" isn't a promise. Besides, when I went into the bedroom there was something else to deal with.

Mrs. Skinner had eaten very little of her breakfast. Her face was flushed and when I felt her forehead it was burning up. Now what should I do? The doctor would be on the road—no way to reach him. The next person I thought of was Mr. Ryan and when I got him on the phone he asked me if I wanted him to get in touch with Dr. Wilkins.

"I don't think so," I said. "Doctor Byford's on his way home."

"You might as well wait then," he said. "Better not to have another stranger right now. Just give her aspirin, Lois, and try to get her to drink liquids."

With that advice to go on, I called Dev again. She'd already told Mr. Emmett she'd like to leave early. She'd come as soon as she could get away.

"Don't worry," I said. "I can do as much for your mother as you can."

I didn't mean that just the way it sounded, but anyhow I spent the rest of the morning at Mrs. Skinner's bedside armed with fruit juice and aspirin.

Along about midday, Harve brought Betsy back. He had Neena with him. She bounced out of the car and announced that she planned to spend the afternoon with me. "I've missed having you at home, Lois," she said. "Besides, it's time I met Dev's mother. You can drive me home tonight."

When I told her Mrs. Skinner was sick, it didn't bother her a bit. "Well, then," she said, "let's go right up to see her."

To tell you the truth I was darn glad Neena had come. In spite of my telling Dev not to worry, I wasn't really comfortable in a sickroom. I told Harve I'd take him back to the house or wherever he wanted to go if he'd wait a few minutes. He said he would. That much about Harve hadn't changed. He still liked to save his legs.

Who knows how it would have gone if Dev's mother had been up and around, feeling good, but when I introduced her to "my grandmother Appleby" she nodded and said, "How do you do?" I guess she was just too miserable to say anything else. Anyhow, Neena has a way with people, and in a few minutes she was putting cool towels on Mrs. Skinner's forehead and whispering soft comforts. "We'll have you feeling better in no time," she said. "Bed is no place to be on a hot summer day."

The "patient" submitted to the care and even came up with a weak smile.

They wouldn't miss me I was sure, and with a promise to be back soon, I went downstairs to Harve who was waiting at the door.

"I want to talk to you," he said as we went down the front steps. "I just found out you wanted to go back to school this fall. Neena told me. She also told me why you can't."

"So?"

"You oughta have the money the folks want to spend on me. Next Saturday night I start on drums with The Rhythm Makers over in North Platte. Of course, I'll just be filling in, but it may lead to a solid spot by September. You know that's what I really want. And some day to have a swing band of my own."

"Thanks, Harve, but no. I've given this a lot of thought lately, and I can see things better now. Dad wants you to have what he didn't have. You've got to give it a try for his sake. That doesn't mean you have to forget your music. Drumming won't go out of style."

"Maybe we'll talk about it again," he said. "I know what it's like to want something real bad. Did you know Neena tried to get a loan on her house in Parker to get money for you?"

"Oh, no. She shouldn't have done that." Neena and her "private matter."

"The bank turned her down and now she's talking about selling her place, coming to live with the folks."

"Boy," I said. "I seem to be turning the whole family upside down, and I don't want that. I tell you, Harve, life sure is complicated."

After that brilliant observation, I drove the rest of the way in a blue funk. Harve said Mom had gone off someplace with Buzz, and I didn't bother to go in the house. I just dropped him off. It was nice to know both Neena and Harve were ready to go to bat for me even if I couldn't accept their offers. And it really surprised me about Harve. Anyhow I shouldn't be so glum. When things got straightened out with Dev and her mother, I'd get out and look for another job.

Up on The Hill again I found Dr. Byford's Studebaker parked in the driveway. He must have arrived just a few minutes after Harve and I took off, because he was in the front hall with Neena and apparently about ready to leave.

"I'm sure glad to see you," I said. "You know my grandmother, don't you? And how's Mrs. Skinner?"

"First of all Mrs. Skinner will be all right in a day or two. She's just got a touch of summer flu. There's a lot of it around. She still doesn't seem to know me, but right now she isn't up to throwing me out. And yes, I know your grandmother. In fact, I've asked her if she'd sort of keep an eye on my patient for the next few days. Not that you and Devonna can't manage, but an experienced hand is always a boon. Besides Mrs. Skinner seems to like your grandmother and that's half the battle."

Neena gave him a "thank you" smile and said, "I was about to tell the doctor I'd be delighted to lend a hand here. Your father won't let me go back to my own house until the end of the week, and I need something to do."

"That's settled then," said Doctor Byford. "I don't imagine you'd want to spend the nights here, Mrs. Appleby, but Dev has told me Bill Emmett picks her up every morning. I'm sure he'd be happy to bring you along when he comes. I'll arrange it with him. Now I'd better get home myself. Haven't been there yet."

I thanked him for stopping by, walked him to his car, and then came back to tell Neena how welcome she was. I also scolded her for trying to dig up money for me. "You are not to do anything foolish."

She just tossed her head and said she wasn't finished yet.

It was too hot to think much about food, but we made some fruit salad and fixed iced tea. Neena took a bowl of chicken broth up to Mrs. Skinner, and when Dev came home we put a card table out on the front porch. It had been such a busy day, and I remembered Dev didn't know about my conversation with Cora. I'd tell her while we ate. In fact, I was just about to when the phone rang. Dev went in to answer it and after a minute she called out to me, "It's long distance. Evanston."

"That's Cora," I called back. "You talk to her. I'll explain later."

It wasn't long before Dev was back outdoors. "She thought she was talking to you," she said, "called me Lois. But she's coming! Here. Thursday. The Flier will drop her off at the station at five-forty-eight." Dev shook her head as though she didn't believe it. "Lois Appleby, how did you pull that off? You are a genius."

"Of course," I said. "Are you just finding that out?"

22.

Now it was just a matter of waiting. First of all, for Mrs. Skinner to get better, which she did with rest and tender care. As Doctor Byford had suggested, Neena came up each morning with Mr. Emmett. She knew Dev's mother was "nineteen," and for the most part she played it that way. She called her Mrs. Skinner, though, not Malvina, and I'm sure it was intentional because on the first morning she said to me, "Back in her mind, Lois, that woman knows who she is."

Well, maybe. Anyhow Mrs. Skinner didn't say anything about it—didn't question it—and the two of them seemed to get along. Once I found them laughing together. Whether it was something in the book they were sharing or some joke between them I don't know. I only know that Mrs. Skinner said, "Your grandmother is so good to me."

Although Neena was at her patient's beck and call, she also found time to take over in the kitchen. Neena loves to cook and these weeks with my mother had cramped her style. All this helped cut down on my chores, and with time on my hands I turned to sewing again, altered two more of Mrs. Skinner's dresses. I couldn't ask her to try them on, but I did have the dotted swiss as a guide.

On Tuesday and Wednesday Dev went off to work but with a difference. She seemed reluctant to leave, and she called two or three times a day to see if her mother was all right. Doctor Byford dropped by once or twice, of course, but right now he was simply treating Mrs. Skinner's flu.

Naturally there was something else we were waiting for and with less patience—at least on my part. The arrival of Mrs. Collingsworth. The train she was coming on didn't make regular stops in small towns like Bannister, but if arrangements were made beforehand passengers would be dropped off.

Dev and Neena and I had debated whether to tell Mrs. Skinner that Cora was coming, but the doctor advised us not to. "Surprise might be the best course." I agreed with him, but one way or the other I could hardly wait to see how it all turned out. Dev wasn't optimistic, though, and told me not to expect too much.

On Thursday we woke up to rain. It wasn't any cooler and the moisture made it twice as muggy, but at least it was a change. After Neena arrived and Dev left, the morning simply dragged. Mrs. Skinner stayed in her room until lunch was over and then, dressed but still looking a little pale, she came downstairs. I noticed that her hair was combed the way it used to be—pulled into a bun low on the back of her neck. I thought maybe that was Neena's doing but she said no. Mrs. Skinner had done it up herself. Hmm.

The two of them wound up in the living room and spent the long afternoon at the piano, sorting out sheet music. I thought how great it was to have Neena with us. When I told her we intended to bring Mrs. Collingsworth back to the house for the evening and probably for the night, she was a step ahead of me.

"I'm planning a pot roast," she said. "I know it's hot for an oven meal, but it's a special occasion."

It was all settled that I was to meet Cora and then swing by Emmett's to pick up Dev when she got off work. That way the three of us would arrive at The Hill together. I don't know how I got through the day. But between pacing the floor and watching the clock I managed.

It was still raining when I left the house, and I'd allowed plenty of time. Bannister's train station isn't right in town. You have to go practically to the end of Main Street and then turn off toward the highway and up a little rise. So there I was just tooling along with the windshield wipers clicking, my hands on the wheel and my mind on Cora Collingsworth. I knew from her letter and the phone conversation that she was a person who came right to the point and had a sense of humor. I had no idea what she looked like. I hadn't seen any pictures, and in all my talking with Malvina, I'd had no description. Of course, if Malvina had described her friend, it would have been as she was in school, without the added years. No matter. She was coming and that was enough.

I was pretty well through town at this point in my daydreaming, almost to the end of the street.

Then I saw it. The yellow roadster! That jazzy little sports car I didn't think I'd ever see again. I couldn't believe it, but there it was, parked diagonally in front of the hotel. I squinted through the rain-spattered glass. No mistake. The top was up now and the isinglass curtains were snapped into place, but it was the yellow roadster all right. This time I looked at the license. I pulled in alongside of it. There was no one behind the wheel, but even as I turned off my motor the guy came out of the hotel. Looking pretty dapper in his seersucker slacks and white polo shirt, he paused in the doorway while he tucked a piece of paper into his pocket. Then he looked around. He saw me all right, probably recognized Betsy. He didn't even have a hat, but the rain seemed as unimportant to him as the dust had that other day. He actually sauntered to the passenger side of my car, rapped on the window, and then opened the door and slid in next to me.

"Hi, Curlyhead." He was just as breezy as he'd been that first time.

"Well," I said, "if it isn't the Mayor of Lodi. What in the world are you doing here?"

The corners of that Clark Gable mouth curled up around the mustache. "I told you I'd see you again some rainy day. It certainly is raining. I thought you might need an umbrella. I was in the hotel asking how to find you."

"I have an umbrella," I said, remembering with irritation that he had accused me of being unprepared. He was so cocky. At the same time I also remembered that I knew something he didn't know I knew. I'd get back at him. "Did you get bored in Evanston?"

I surprised him all right. His eyebrows shot up and he said, "What do you use, a crystal ball or Pinkertons?"

"I even know your real name. Paul—Paul Collingsworth."

"Okay, ten points for your side," he said, "but there has to be an explanation. Let's have it."

That was only fair, and I started by telling him about my

167

staying with my friend, Dev, and why. When I got to the letter, I said, "That bit about the yellow car cinched it. Who else could you be? Boy, it sure would have saved us some time if you'd told me who you were that day on the road *and* that you'd been up to The Hill."

"Hey," he said, "I wasn't about to admit I'd been at that house. That woman! And I don't care what she means to you or that she's my mother's friend. She scared the daylights out of me. When she opened the door she gave me one shocked look as though I'd come from some other planet. I introduced myself and started to tell her why I was there, but I don't think she was listening. She kept staring at me. I couldn't figure out what was going on in her mind. Then all at once she was very friendly, just took over the conversation. Most of what she said was beyond me, something about school and when would the wedding be. I couldn't get out of there fast enough."

"And she called you Tru, didn't she?"

"Yes, she did, but it wasn't until later I realized she must have had some crazy idea I was my father."

"Wait a minute. Your father?"

"Sure. My real father."

"Truman McChesney?" It was falling into place.

"That's right. Collingsworth is my stepfather. He adopted me and I've always called him Dad. I never knew McChesney. He was killed in the early action of the war. He'd gone overseas with a Canadian outfit in 1914. I was only a baby. I've seen pictures. I guess I do look like him."

So Dev's mother thought she was seeing the man who was engaged to her friend, Cora. But would that have been enough to turn her mind back? I could see Paul Collingsworth was still confused and was waiting for me to say more. I obliged.

168

"You see we felt you had something to do with what happened to Mrs. Skinner," I said, "and we figured, in the beginning, that is, that if we could get you to see her again . . ."

"I don't think you could have convinced me to do that. Besides she's my mother's friend. Maybe it's my mother you need."

Now it was my turn to be cocky. "It's your mother we've got," I said. "Would you believe I was on my way to meet her when I saw your car?" I looked at my watch. "And even though I gave myself loads of time, I'd better not waste any more of it. Otherwise, she'll be stranded at the station."

23.

There were a few other things I needed to explain, but the upshot of it was that Paul Collingsworth followed me to the train station in the yellow roadster. It seemed to be the logical thing to do. Logical? That was a laugh. Nothing was logical anymore. A month ago when this guy stopped to fix my tire on the highway, who would have dreamed that today we'd be here together in Bannister and on the way to meet his mother! Well, "take it in stride." That's what Neena always tells me. We were sure enough heading for the station, and from the hotel it took us only five minutes to get there.

Bannister's depot is certainly nothing to brag about, a brown frame box of a building right alongside the tracks. There's a stationmaster on duty all hours of the day and night, but except for freight and the mail, most of the trains just zoom on by us. The waiting room has a ticket window and several wooden benches, and now that summer is on us a ceiling fan does its best to keep the air moving. Today it would have a hard time, rain or not.

We parked and got out of our cars with still a few minutes to spare. Paul sort of stayed in the background. He said it was my show and he didn't want to get in the spotlight. At five-forty-eight, on the nose, the Flier ground to a stop, and almost at once Mrs. Collingsworth and her blue leather overnight case were deposited on the platform. If you'd been counting you wouldn't have made it to twelve before the train moved on again with a spurt of steam.

Since Cora was the only passenger to get off she didn't need to wear a rose, but I'm sure I could have picked her out of a crowd. Neena would have called her an aristocrat. It's hard for me to imagine anyone having money. Most of the people I know were hard hit by the depression and still groaning. I was sure this woman, who held out a white-gloved hand to me, had never pinched a penny.

"You have to be Lois," she said, "and you are just what I expected."

"I hope that's good," I said, but I knew she meant it as a compliment. I wanted to say she was even more than I expected. She was tall and willowy with a firm chin and an easy smile. The brim of her blue hat dipped at just the right angle over dark eyes, and the navy piqué suit was trim cut and with a hemline exactly the proper number of inches above matching pumps. She was elegant. Still, what else would she be? Wasn't she the mother of the collar ad?

I welcomed her to Bannister and thanked her for coming.

"You can thank yourself," she said. "You're the one who brought me here. To track me down and to call me as you did was most resourceful. I should never have let the years go by when I didn't hear from Mookie. But it didn't occur to me that there could be anything really wrong, and the time just got away from me. And to think I might have just waited for a reply to my letter. No, my dear, I should be thanking you."

I was a little uncomfortable with such praise and said after all I had called with Mrs. Skinner's daughter's approval. "And Dev would be here now but she's at work."

As we talked I saw Mrs. Collingsworth glance beyond me and I knew she had spotted her son.

"You needn't hide from me, Paul," she said. "I have absolutely no idea how you happen to be here, but it doesn't surprise me to see that you have found a good-looking girl to keep you company."

Paul laughed, and I felt a little embarrassed.

I suggested that if we could do without comfort we could sit in the waiting room while we got our stories together. Paul took only a minute or two to explain his presence, and then I went over what I'd said on the phone, putting in some details. Mrs. Collingsworth listened with what seemed like real interest. Once she said, "Poor Mookie," and when I'd finished, her eyes filled with tears. Finally, I looked at my watch and said we'd better get along.

Mrs. Collingsworth rode with me and the yellow roadster tailed Betsy again as we headed for Emmett's.

Dev was waiting for us out in front, and I could tell she was excited now too, in spite of her earlier pessimism.

After the necessary introductions and Dev's surprise that we had Paul with us, Mrs. Collingsworth said what a pleasure it was to meet the daughter of her old friend. "I'm glad you abbreviated your name to Dev, though. I remember when your mother sent me the announcement I was horrified that a five-pound babe should be weighted down with 'Devonnabelle'."

"Mama's never shortened it," said Dev. "She still calls me
. . ." She caught herself and stopped.

"I understand, my dear," said Mrs. Collingsworth. "Lois has
explained the situation. Let's hope I can be of help."

We talked for a minute or two about the problem and then
Mrs. Collingsworth said if we didn't mind she was anxious to
see Mookie and could we go.

It was Paul who came up with the idea that Dev should drive
Betsy and take his mother. "That way the two of them can get
acquainted," he said, "and if I'm invited, Curlyhead, I'll give
you a ride."

Naturally, I said he was invited and I agreed to the riding
arrangement. As I handed Dev my keys, I whispered, "I didn't
tell Cora about your father. I think you should, though. She
knew him too."

Even though I remembered that Paul had been to the Skinner
house before, I gave him brief directions. Then I settled in beside him, thinking what a strange chance put me here. I liked
it.

"Did I tell you," I said, "that I was glad to see you?"

"No, you didn't. As a matter of fact, I seemed to be just a
small background bit of sky in the jigsaw puzzle you were working
on. Not very flattering."

"Under the circumstances you can't blame me for that. I never
expected to see you again."

"In retrospect," he said, "you grew on me. You know I actually got to thinking how great it would be if you'd take your—
geology wasn't it?—at Tucson."

"Hmph," I almost snorted. "Right now, it doesn't look as
though I'm going to take it anywhere." I told him the things
that had happened.

"I'm sorry," he said, sounding as though he really was. "School was just handed to me, I guess. Not out of my dad's pocket either, although he said he'd be glad to foot the bill. My own father's inheritance, modest as it was, came to me. It's seeing me through."

So Paul Collingsworth could go to college twice if he wanted to. We were from different worlds, I could see that. All the same, he'd come to Bannister *just to see me.*

The roadster got to The Hill first. Maybe Dev drove slowly in order to have more time to visit with Cora. I certainly hoped it wasn't because she got scared and wanted to put off the meeting as long as possible.

We parked in the front drive and waited until Betsy pulled in beside us. Dev said she'd see if this would be a good time to surprise her mother. She got to the door just as Neena was on her way out to tell us that everything was fine. Mrs. Skinner was in the living room much as I had left her. She was going through the music again. "I'll tell her she has company."

The time had come. It sounds corny to say that, but nothing else fits. We all trooped into the house, Paul and I hanging back a bit but not so far back that we couldn't see and hear. I wouldn't miss this for the world.

When Neena made her announcement, Mrs. Skinner lifted her head from the pile of sheet music she held and her eyes must have met those of her friend.

"Surprise," said Cora. "Well, Mookie, don't you know me?"

Oh boy! *Should she have used that nickname?* But I hadn't asked her not to and naturally she would. Mrs. Skinner had always been Mookie to her, no matter that they were no longer girls.

I don't know whether I can describe the expression on Mrs. Skinner's face—maybe because one gave way to another so quickly.

She was startled to begin with. Then there was question, then disbelief, then finally, yes, pleasure. I was sure. My knees were actually trembling. You would have thought this was the most important moment of my life. How deeply I had become involved with Mrs. Skinner.

"Well." Cora again. "I finally found Bannister on the map and here I am. Have I changed all that much?"

Mrs. Skinner got to her feet and the sheet music slid to the floor. "Cora, Cora," she said. Her voice was a little high-pitched, but I couldn't tell for sure whether or not it was the voice of Malvina. She took a step or two toward her friend and then the two women were in each other's arms.

Was she greeting her schoolgirl roommate? Or was it her long-time friend from Evanston, the friend she hadn't seen for twenty years?

They hugged each other for what seemed a lifetime. Dev moved closer to her mother. I joined Neena, and Paul stayed where he was—all of us waiting. At last Mrs. Skinner backed off and was the first to speak. "Cora," she said, "it's so good to see you."

That could be from either world I thought. Which one is she in?

"It's good to see you too, Mookie," said Cora. "And what's more . . ." She motioned for Paul. "I brought . . ."

"Tru," interrupted Mrs. Skinner. "Of course."

"No. No," Cora shot back. "Not Tru. That was long ago. Tru's gone. You remember. This is my son."

There was a terrible look on Mrs. Skinner's face. The same look she'd had the night of the carnival. She put her hand to her head and in a voice barely audible said, "Something is dreadfully wrong." Then she seemed suddenly to wilt.

Dev took hold of her mother's elbow and led her to a chair.

24.

I don't know about the others, but I wilted right along with Mrs. Skinner. I guess I had expected too much.

Cora went to her friend at once and said softly, "Take a minute. You'll see. Things will be clear."

Dev, with her arm around her mother's shoulder, echoed the assurance while Mrs. Skinner just sat there rubbing her forehead as though to wipe away whatever it was that was dreadfully wrong. Finally she moistened her lips and said, "Forgive me. For a moment I was confused."

Cora said, "You're fine now, Mookie. Fine."

Mrs. Skinner didn't look at all sure. Still, when she spoke again her voice was stronger. "But your son is the image of Tru, you know."

Oh glory!

I was sure everyone could hear my heart thumping as Cora said, "It's about time you met him. And I've been anxious to meet Devonnabelle."

Mrs. Skinner followed Cora's gaze to Dev and for the longest time she seemed to study her face. At last she said, "Yes, Devonnabelle, my daughter."

Her daughter! I wanted to shout it. Then Mrs. Skinner looked up at Neena and me, and I was uneasy again. I didn't think she'd be surprised that I was there. After all I'd been on The Hill off and on during the past years. Neena was the one she might not be able to fit into the picture. But Dev handled it. Even though there had been hasty introductions out on the porch she repeated them.

"Mrs. Collingsworth, Paul," she said, "this is Lois's grandmother. Mama's had a touch of the flu and Mrs. Appleby was kind enough to look after her for a few days."

Mrs. Skinner gave Dev a bewildered glance, and Neena promptly changed the subject.

"I'm sure everyone is hungry," she said, "and if Lois will give me a hand we can sit down to eat in a few minutes."

I didn't really want to leave the others now that things were moving so fast, but it was only natural for Neena to call on me. One nice thing, Paul tagged along to the kitchen, and I didn't mind that.

"You sure didn't know," I said, "that you were going to get in on a Skinner crisis. Are you sorry you came?"

"Certainly not. Especially since I didn't have to take care of it. Besides I've always enjoyed seeing my mother in action. Dad says she's a cross between a playwright and a politician with a little bit of faith healer thrown in."

"I'm not sure that's a compliment. Does your mother mind the description?"

"Oh, she knows it's a compliment. Anyhow he also says she

has a first class ticket to heaven tucked away in her pocketbook."

"I like your dad."

While we talked I made short work of setting the table, and under Neena's direction Paul and I carried the bowls and platters into the dining room. I guess I hadn't missed anything important. Dev gave me a nod of reassurance as she ushered her mother and Cora to the table, and Cora was saying, apparently in answer to a question, "It really doesn't matter what prompted my visit, Mookie. I've been thinking about you and just got an urge to see you."

While we enjoyed Neena's good food, the conversation kept everybody at attention and me on the edge of my chair.

At the beginning Cora wisely avoided both ends of Mrs. Skinner's life from the Lindenwood days until now. She talked instead of the years in the middle—those Christmas card years when she and Mookie didn't see each other.

"It's just shameful," she said, "that we never got together, but as they say, it takes more time to raise an only chick than it does a brood. Both of us were in that position, and the years just rolled by. I knew you were as busy as I was."

I kept a close watch on Mrs. Skinner. I admit I was a little bit afraid, but she seemed to be okay. Although she didn't have much to say she put in a word or two. Nothing more was necessary. Cora did most of the talking. Still she had a way of pulling us toward her, drawing us out so that no one would feel neglected. Sometimes it was with a question. "Where is your home, Mrs. Appleby? Lois said you were just here for a short stay." Sometimes with a compliment. "You have such lovely hands, Dev. You must be a pianist too. I always loved to hear your mother play." Of course, when a response was called for she allowed time for it. She asked me if I'd ever been to Chicago, and I told her I hated to admit it but I'd never been east of Grand Island.

She laughed and said, "There's always tomorrow. Besides, you may have the better part. A small town is certainly much more friendly, and from what I've seen of Bannister, even in the rain, it's charming."

More diplomat than politician, I thought, as she shifted the talk of her husband and her son.

"Jack's working too hard," she said. "He has his hand in a number of business ventures, some of which I know nothing about. I must say he's solvent, and, of course, he's still hanging on to his insurance company. Paul has one more year at the University of Arizona. It was such good fortune that the doctor suggested he spend his college years in a dry climate. All the while he was growing up we battled that bronchial problem. He's ever so much better now."

"Arizona's a good school," said Paul, getting in his word.

That was when Mrs. Skinner said, "I had hoped that Devonnabelle would go to Lindenwood, but . . ."

She faltered and Dev came to the rescue, breaking into the sentence. "I guess I'm just a homebody. I didn't want to leave Bannister."

Neena had a quick response to that although she avoided my eyes. "There's nothing wrong with homemaking as a career," she said. When it came to diplomacy, little Neena stood just as tall as Mrs. Collingsworth.

Finally and gradually, the talk inched back to those school days when Malvina had been happy, and I really began to worry.

"Do you remember Hazel Blodgett, the drama major?" said Cora, "and how we banished her to the basement storeroom to do her emoting?"

"It was that or pass out earmuffs," said Mrs. Skinner with surprising good humor. And she went right on. "Hazel's roommate was the one who used to bother me. Always wanting to borrow my clothes."

"Lottie, yes. Lottie Lupin. We called her the rabbit."

No one else at the table was talking. We were all engrossed in the reminiscences of these two women who had been so long apart. Mrs. Skinner was now holding up her end of the conversation, and Dev and I kept looking at each other. We were the ones who most understood what was at stake. But nothing happened. Dozens of old memories were pulled out and relived. And the important thing was that they were *re*lived. Mrs. Skinner was looking back on them.

There was one subject, though, that had been skirted. Dev's father. I had a feeling Cora would get to it. She seemed determined to touch on everything before the evening was over.

It was after dessert and coffee that she said, "Do you remember, Mookie, the night I went to St. Louis to some dance with Tru? His dad had just presented him with one of Henry Ford's flivvers. We had to try it out on the road."

"How could I forget? We were only sophomores and didn't have much freedom. I know I had to sneak down long after the door was bolted to let you in. It must have been three o'clock. But the worst part, you wouldn't let me go back to bed."

"There was so much to talk about. Tru wanted me to quit school, get married, and go off to Australia with him. But you had things to tell me too, Mookie. That was the night you met Henry."

There it was. Cora had tossed the hot potato. And Mrs. Skinner? Well, she caught it and held it as long as was necessary. "Yes, that was the night," she said quite calmly. Then with the same even voice, "By the way did I ever tell you he came out to Bannister during that Christmas holiday to meet my father?"

"Of course, you did. We told each other everything. Oh, Henry was smitten all right. But you also told me your father didn't like him."

"He made no secret of that." I could almost see Mrs. Skinner going back over the years in her mind, and there was pain in her eyes. "Father said Henry didn't know how to cope with the real world and certainly didn't have a head for business."

So, I thought, Ace Cameron didn't like Henry Skinner. And from the very beginning. Was that why Malvina's life started to sour?

"But it was such a handsome head," Cora retorted. "and one thing sure, after Henry met you he never looked at another girl. He didn't look for adventure either. I didn't have that kind of devotion from Tru. He had a wanderlust which had to be satisfied with or without me."

A dark brooding look had come over Mrs. Skinner's face. She put her hand on her friend's arm, and I could see it was a tight grip. "Oh, Cora," she said, and her lips quivered. "Father was right I'm afraid. The most dreadful thing happened."

Dev shot a look at me—one of amazement. *Was she going to talk about it?*

Cora covered Mrs. Skinner's hand with her own and said gently, "I know what happened, Mookie. Dev told me everything. You should have written to me at the time. Maybe I could have helped. We always helped each other. You know that. I certainly leaned on you when Tru left."

Mrs. Skinner was looking straight ahead, her eyes misty, as Cora went on, "It's in the past now—over. Don't hold onto it. We all have some kind of trouble. You knew mine. Tru running off to Canada to fight a war, a war we weren't even in yet, leaving me with an infant."

I think Cora saw me glance at Paul and she added quickly, "I'm happy to say Paul seems to have inherited Tru's best qualities. And I suppose I was to blame too. As you very well know, I did quit school to marry him in January of that sophomore year. I shouldn't have. We didn't go to Australia, of course, had a baby instead." Cora settled the warmest of smiles on Paul. "I was glad for that afterwards. Just remember, Mookie, things have a way of working out—in time."

There was such a silence.

At last Mrs. Skinner released her hold on Cora's arm. The tension was relieved.

We had been sitting around the table for at least two hours, and I guess Cora had brought up all she intended to.

"I've gone on long enough for one night," she said, "and if you've had the flu, Mookie, you'd better get to bed."

Mrs. Skinner said, "Yes, I am tired."

Dev pushed her chair back and got up. "Mrs. Collingsworth, you'll stay on awhile, won't you?" she said, asserting herself as the hostess. "You can talk more tomorrow."

"Fine," said Cora, "but I can stay only until Saturday. Jack's in Hartford for a board meeting. I called him before I left and promised to be home by Sunday morning."

On that we moved into the living room. Neena said she'd clean up in the kitchen, but Dev put her foot down. "You've done your share. Lois and I can take care of things."

"Very well then," said Neena. "Perhaps I'd better get back to town. I should spend a little more time with Lois's mother. I won't be coming up in the morning with Mr. Emmett. I'll call him. Everyone here seems to be in good health now." Dev and I knew she was referring to more than a bout with the flu.

"I have a suggestion," said Mrs. Collingsworth. "As long as the girls are doing kitchen duty, why can't Paul run Mrs. Appleby home? He wouldn't be any help with the dishes anyhow."

Paul took Neena's arm and said she had a treat in store for her. "It isn't everyone who gets a ride in my yellow lemonsine."

"I'll see you tomorrow, Neena," I said. "Thank you for being here. I'll take you to Parker whenever you're ready."

When they had gone, Mrs. Collingsworth said she was a bit tired too, and Dev went upstairs with her mother and Cora to see about the rooms.

Later, while we worked in the kitchen, we talked about the evening.

"Lois," said Dev, "I can't believe it. We're having houseguests—houseguests, mind you. And there was more laughter and life here on The Hill tonight than we've had for years. I just can't believe it."

There was something else that was hard to believe. Mrs. Skinner had not reverted to the zombielike person she had been since Henry Skinner's suicide. Nor had she snapped back to the cold, forbidding woman she had been before that. She was gentler, more pleasant. How had it happened? Had Cora brought about the change? Cora, a confidante, a friend—something Mrs. Skinner had never allowed herself to look for in Bannister?

Or had being nineteen-year-old Malvina once again subconsciously affected her? Perhaps I'd never know.

25.

Both Mrs. Skinner and Cora had gone to bed, and Dev and I had finished the dishes before Paul came back. He said my grandmother had insisted on taking him into the house and introducing him around, late as it was. Knowing Neena, I was sure she'd given him a run down on the family history as well. He also said it had stopped raining, and he was all for going out—the three of us—finding something to do.

"I don't know what it would be," said Dev, "but you and Lois run along if you want."

I really wanted to go, but it didn't seem right to leave Dev by herself. I begged off too, and we simply sat out on the porch for awhile just as we had that night with Ben. No, I take that back. It was not the same. For one thing Dev wasn't in her nightgown. For another I was sitting there next to Paul Collingsworth getting goose bumps. I never got goose bumps with Ben Oldham.

I think we all had our separate thoughts, and we didn't talk much. After an hour or so, Dev showed Paul his room, and we all turned in.

The next morning, Dev and I were the first ones up. She wanted to call Doctor Byford before she left for work. He was pleased to hear about her mother and said we'd just keep our fingers crossed for awhile—trust that she stayed on course. "I'll come to see her when the company's gone. Let me know if you need me."

I suggested Dev call Mr. Emmett too. He wouldn't have to pick her up this morning. I'd see that she got to the store.

The telephoning was barely out of the way when Mrs. Collingsworth and Paul came downstairs.

"I'm sorry to be dashing off," said Dev, "but I'll see you tonight. I do want you to know how I appreciate your coming and what you've done for us."

"I did only what it was my pleasure to do," said Cora. "I'm happy that it worked out as it did."

"Just make yourselves at home. There's a pot of coffee on the stove and plenty of eggs, cereal, bread for toast."

"Don't be concerned," said Cora. "We're in no hurry for breakfast. I'd rather wait for your mother anyhow."

I didn't dare to think it was possible that Mrs. Skinner's recovery hadn't lasted through the night, but all I said was that I'd be back very soon.

It was another of those worries I needn't have had. In a matter of minutes and before Dev and I left, she appeared in the kitchen. She was pretty much as she had been at bedtime and had on one of the dresses I had altered for her while she was sick.

When Cora said how nice she looked she said, "You know,

Cora, I lost so much weight. Very few of my clothes fit me. Only two or three things have been taken in. I'll have to see to the rest of them or get something new."

She didn't remember I'd been sewing for her.

On the way to Emmett's, Dev and I talked about her mother, and I said it wasn't necessary for me to be staying with her anymore. She was even so much better than she had been before she popped back to 1913.

"But you've got to stay on," said Dev. "I'd be lost without you."

"I don't belong there now. You have to be by yourselves again, you and your mother. I'll stay just until Cora and Paul leave. It's better that way."

After I let Dev out at the store, I decided since I hadn't seen or talked to Mom for a few days, I'd stop by just to say hello. I knew Neena would have told her all about Mrs. Skinner's visitors and probably how everything turned out, but I sort of wanted her to hear it from me.

I saw Neena and Buzz puttering around in the patch of garden by the side fence, and I found Mom in the kitchen baking for the weekend. Mom will bake no matter how hot it gets.

"Hi," I said, "what's new?"

"Not much, dear," she said as she took two pans of honey buns out of the oven. "I guess you know your grandmother is going home Sunday. It seems she's hardly been here at all, but I understand her wanting to get back to her own home. Your father and I will drive up with her after church."

"Unless you really want to make the trip," I said, "I'll take her. I've already mentioned it to her. But how about Harve? When's he leaving? He told me he got that job with the band in North Platte." I realized when I said it that this was probably a sore spot, but she seemed cheerful enough when she answered.

"He's leaving this afternoon. Chuck's taking him—actually going with him. They're down at the garage now getting Chuck's car gassed up. They plan to get a room together. It will be a nice summer experience for the boys."

The way she emphasized "summer" I knew Harve had given in and was set for school in September. "If I don't see them before they go," I said, "tell Harve to hang in there. I'm proud of him."

I started to tell Mom about Mrs. Skinner, but she said she knew. She didn't seem to want to hear about it again.

"I didn't approve of your being involved with that business, Lois, but I always thought Devonna was a nice girl. I'm glad for her sake everything's going to be all right."

"I'm glad too," I said, which was the understatement of the year.

Mom slid two more pans of rolls into the oven and then said, "I suppose you'll be able to come home now that your mission is accomplished."

I wouldn't have called it a mission, but I said, "I expect so. If I take Neena to Parker, though, I may stay with her for awhile."

Mom must have thought I was still hurt about the money thing because she said, "I'm sorry we weren't able to offer you the help you wanted for school, Lois. You understand, don't you?"

"I do, Mom. Don't worry about it."

"Do you have any plans yet for fall? You should try for another school, dear. I can't help thinking how foolish you were to leave your job in Spring Willow."

I didn't answer that. Darn it, she was the one who didn't understand. Then when I said, "I'd better get along," she thrust a pan of warm honey buns into my hands.

"Take these to the Skinners," she said.

"Thanks. I'm sure they'll enjoy them." Mom means well.

I stopped by the garden and Neena accepted my offer of a ride to Parker. And by all means I must stay with her for awhile. "You know it has occurred to me," she said, "you might find a summer job up there. We'll look around."

When I told Buzz I'd be home tomorrow, he asked about Mrs. Skinner.

"She's better, Buzz." I was glad I didn't have to explain.

"She told me I could come back to The Hill anytime I wanted and play in the yard—maybe build a tree house. Can I go, even if you're not there?"

It was a good question, but I said, "I don't see why not. You can sure ask her." It might be the first test for the new Mrs. Skinner.

As I drove away, I realized my visit with Mom only brought me head on with a real worry. Now that Dev's need for me was gone, I was right back where I'd been when I came home from Spring Willow. No job, no school—no Ben. Goose bumps or not, maybe I should tell Ben I'd changed my mind and settle for home and family as Neena had done. No. No. No. I knocked that choice down in a hurry, for Ben's sake as well as mine. He needed a good farm wife, and that I could never be. He'd find someone better. It looked as though I didn't fit in anyplace. Even on The Hill I was no longer the hired girl.

Breakfast was over when I got back, and Mrs. Skinner and Cora were sharing duties. They also seemed to have picked up the threads of last night's conversation. I stayed pretty much out of the way, and when Paul suggested I show him the country-side, I jumped at the chance.

The top on the roadster was down again, and in spite of the heat we had fun. The rain had washed away the dust, and the meadowlarks were at their best. We drove past the new grain elevator and out to Massacre Bluff which boasts Bannister's one historic monument. We saw the young cornfields and the winter wheat which would be turning from green to gold very soon now. In town I pointed out our little library and the bank. He'd already seen the hotel. Of course, we stopped at Ryan's. I wanted to tell Mr. Ryan what had happened and that it looked as though everything might be all right with Dev's mother. We sat up at the counter and had a lemon phosphate, and then since we had run out of things to see we went back to the house. Paul said he'd talked to my dad last night about the brakes on the road-ster. "If I'm heading out through the Rockies I want good brakes. Your dad said to come in this afternoon and he'd have a look at them."

It worked out that when Paul did go off to the garage and while Mrs. Skinner was resting, I had a chance for some time alone with Mrs. Collingsworth.

I told her what Doctor Byford had said about keeping our fingers crossed, and then I asked her how she felt. Did she think Dev's mother would be all right now?

"The doctor's the one to tell you that," she said, "but for my part I think she'll be fine. I'll certainly keep in close touch with her from now on. And with Dev. You know Mookie is so fortunate to have a daughter. I've told her that. I always wanted a girl—a girl too, you understand. I wouldn't give up Paul for the world, but you know the old saying. 'A son's a son till he gets him a wife; a daughter's a daughter all of her life.' "

"I don't know about the sons, but you're right about Dev. What would Mrs. Skinner have done without her? You know, though, you're the one who pulled this last thing off. It was wonderful of you to drop everything and come."

"There was a time when the tables were turned, even though Mookie may have forgotten. If it hadn't been for her I might have cracked in those first months when Tru went off adventuring. And later when he was killed. She was still in school and since I lived not far from the campus she spent many a weekend with me. My upheaval came earlier in my life than hers did, but there was something of a parallel. Both of us were abandoned."

As she was talking, more of the jigsaw puzzle, as Paul called it, fell into place. *Here was the key piece.* I could see now why Paul's appearance had made Dev's mother react as she did. Seeing Paul—Tru—took her back to a time before either she or Cora had come to grief. If Tru was around and it was the summer of 1913, everything was rosy.

I pulled myself away from my thoughts and said, "I still think it was great of you to come. I hope I can have a friend like you some day. And that maybe I can be one."

Mrs. Collingsworth drew back in something like surprise.

"But my dear, you already are. Don't you realize that?"

"If you mean my coming up here to The Hill to help out, that wasn't anything."

"I know," she said. "It's never anything when it's from the heart." She reached over and patted my arm. I felt so much at ease with Cora Collingsworth.

I think she felt the need to talk about something else and she said, "Paul told me this morning about your thwarted plans. Do you know what you're going to do now?"

"Not really," I said. "I can still register with the teacher's agency. Sometimes a vacancy comes up the last minute. Otherwise I don't know. I do have some money saved from this last year. Mr. Ryan might still have a job for me, and I can always live at home."

"Hmm," she said thoughtfully. "I'm sure something will work out."

"Neena says that. I wish I had your confidence."

It was almost six when Paul got back and came to find me. "It's no wonder your father hasn't money to loan you for school," he said. "He just did a brake job on my car and charged me about half what it would have been in Chicago."

"Everything's cheaper in a small town," I said. "Besides, that's my dad—if he likes someone. You must have made a good impression."

By six-thirty Dev was home and we gathered around the table again. Neena was missing, though, along with her special touch with food. I had put together an easy meal—sweet corn, cold sliced ham, and fruit. We did have the honey buns Mom sent. They were delicious.

Cora said she would be leaving on the train that came through Bannister at eleven-thirty in the morning. She had checked with the stationmaster. He said he'd flag it down for her. She'd have a sleeper out of Omaha and get into Chicago early Sunday.

Paul said he'd leave in the morning too. He was going to Durango, Colorado, had promised a buddy of his he'd meet him at some dude ranch there. "And I'm already a day late."

"I wish you could stay longer," said Mrs. Skinner. "I hope you'll come again."

"And you, Mookie, you simply must come to Evanston, be

with me for awhile. Dev too, of course. I can't wait to tell Jack about our reunion."

Mrs. Collingsworth's eyes swept around the table and rested on me. "I have a different kind of invitation for Lois. I know you planned to go to the university at Lincoln, but would you consider Northwestern? Illinois is a big oil state. Jack tells me there's been some new discovery just this year."

I must have looked completely confused.

"I guess," she said, "I'm not making myself clear. We're right in Evanston, and we'd love to have you live with us while you go to school. With Paul gone and Jack traveling as he does, I get lonely. We have a fair-sized house and I just rattle around in it."

Finally what she was saying got through my thick skull. "Oh, I couldn't," I said.

"Why not? There would be an outstate tuition fee, of course, but you said you had some money saved, and if you don't have enough for that or for your personal expenses, we could give you a loan. Just a loan. I know you want to be independent."

I was stunned. "I don't know what to say."

"You don't have to say anything right now, my dear. Just think about it. Talk it over with your folks—and your grandmother. She seems to be very important in your life, and I have a feeling she would be on my side."

I think Mrs. Collingsworth could see I was ready to blubber, and she shifted the conversation to something else. Don't ask me what it was. I couldn't get beyond that beautiful invitation.

And I thought last night that things were moving fast.

26.

After Mrs. Collingsworth's offer, a lot of the table talk went right through my head. I was in a daze. Wouldn't you be if what you wanted most in all the world was held out to you like that? You only had to reach for it? Wow! Did people really do this kind of thing? But, of course, I couldn't accept. I was a stranger to the Collingsworths. Well, practically a stranger. No, I couldn't possibly accept, and this reality brought me back from my dreaming.

At the end of the meal, Paul said, "I don't know what the rest of you are doing tonight, but Curlyhead and I are going to a dance in Redmond. There is one. I checked in town this afternoon. Dev, you too, if you want to come. I can handle the two of you—good for my ego."

Dev laughed and said, "Thanks just the same, but this is your mother's last night here. I'll pass."

I could have kissed her. I knew what she was doing. She was letting me have him all to myself. I did help with the dishes and the straightening up in the kitchen before I went to get ready, but by nine o'clock we were off to Redmond in the yellow lemonsine.

On the road we talked and laughed and sang away the twenty miles. Paul asked what we had for excitement in Bannister besides dancing at the Legion Hall in Redmond, and how did we manage without a real ballroom, big league baseball, vaudeville, and a good steak house.

"We can always get a good steak at Johnnie's," I said defensively. "The best. And Bannister's baseball team is better than big league because you know the players personally. As for shows—touring companies come to North Platte every once in awhile, and just last year this guy came out from Denver and put on a musical in our own high school auditorium with local talent. It was great."

"Spare me that joy," he said.

"Besides, we have other things in a small town. Band concerts and picnics and parades and lots of friends. Everybody knows everybody else."

"As well as their business, I imagine."

"I guess it is hard to have any secrets. Right now tongues are probably wagging all over town about you and your mother. What difference does it make?"

"Only kidding," he said. "After all, Bannister does have Lois Appleby."

Later, on the dance floor, I stopped talking. I just relaxed, followed Paul's strong lead and enjoyed.

I'm sure everybody was looking at us, wondering where Lois Appleby found the gorgeous man. We didn't give anybody a chance to ask. Paul let no one cut in, and when somebody would head our way between dances or during intermission, I saw to it that we moved off in another direction.

Neither one of us mentioned school, but over hamburgers and milkshakes before we went home, Paul said, "My mother meant what she said about your living with them while you go to Northwestern. She's the same sort as your dad when she likes someone. Besides, she has a penchant for doing good things. When I was little there was always someone at our house on weekends or during the summer, and she used to borrow the neighbor's kids to take to the park or the zoo. Then when I started at Arizona there was this distant cousin—Jane. Her father was going to have to pull her out of school. He hadn't been able to survive the crash, I guess. She moved out of the dorm and in with the folks—stayed until she graduated."

"But she was a relative," I protested.

"Distant. Besides, that didn't have anything to do with it. Anyone who wants to go to school rings a special bell with my mother—because she didn't finish, I guess."

"Anyhow it was great of her to ask me, even if I can't go."

"Obstinate," he muttered and finished off his shake.

We got back to The Hill very late. I wanted to talk to Dev, but the house was quiet. As a matter of fact, Paul took off his shoes before he went upstairs in order not to wake anyone. I didn't have to be that careful, but I, too, got into bed with as little noise as possible.

It had been a sensational night, and as I lay there, still too excited to be sleepy, I thought back over it. As usual I had babbled on about my childhood, my teaching, my future hopes. Then I checked over what I had found out about Paul. He liked his stepfather, thought his mother was terrific, had one more year at school and was stopping at Durango on his way back to Tucson. Not much more. And all those things I knew before tonight. Okay, so he was a private person. I figure if a guy loves his mother he's all right.

On Saturday morning everyone was up early. Dev didn't go to work. Mr. Emmett said she could come in at noon. We had a leisurely breakfast and then made our plans.

Cora and Paul had to gather their things together, and I had to pack too. I intended to go on home as soon as we saw Cora off. I was glad when Dev came and sat on the bed in my room, while I transferred my belongings from the chest of drawers to my suitcase. Both of us had a lot to say, and for openers she asked how things went last night and did I have a good time?

"Dreamy," I said. "But that guy's not exactly an open book. You'd be surprised how little he told me about himself."

"Is he going to write to you?"

"I'm not counting on it. Anyhow, I've got other things to think of." I told her about going to Parker and maybe looking for a job there.

"I'll sure miss having you here, Lois."

"I'm not going to China," I said. "I'll be around. But things will be better for you now. Wait and see."

"Mama is different somehow. But maybe it's just because her friend's here."

"Maybe. But you're different now too."

"I suppose so. I think I understand Mama more. Still there's this bigger thing. I wonder if she's really well. I mean this won't happen again will it?"

"I guess no one can be sure about that. You can help, though, and with the doctor standing by and Cora keeping in touch. Maybe you can manage to have your mother visit her."

196

"That's pretty improbable right now, but it's something to work toward. I told you before, Lois, I can't begin to pay you back for what you've done. Not only the caring for Mama. I wouldn't have had the courage to call Mrs. Collingsworth. You know that. But if it's going to work out that you'll go to Northwestern, then I feel in a way you are getting paid. You are going, aren't you? I think you should."

"Easy for you to say. I'm sure my folks wouldn't approve."

"Can't you decide for yourself? You're practically twenty-one."

That was something to think about.

I don't know why we assumed that Mrs. Skinner would bid Cora good-bye at the house, but she surprised us all by announcing that she would like to go to the station with us. It would be the first time she'd been off The Hill for I don't know how long. Amazing!

Dev and I exchanged glances, and Cora said, "Of course, you'll see me off. I would insist on it."

Since the roadster had room for only two, I told Dev to take her mother and Mrs. Collingsworth in Betsy. They could squeeze into the front seat. Paul put my suitcase and some odds and ends into the roadster and we were all set.

Word had indeed gone around town about Mrs. Skinner's visitors, and all along Main Street people stared at us or waved. It didn't bother me, but I directed Paul down a side street that brought us out behind the hotel.

As we waited for the train, there were good-byes all around. Between Dev and Mrs. Collingsworth. Between Cora and Mookie, and that was tearful. Between Mrs. Collingsworth and me. Mrs. Collingsworth squeezed my hand and said, "Please say yes to my plan for you. It's selfishness on my part, believe me."

"I know you mean that, but I honestly don't . . ."

She interrupted. "Stop right there. Don't say no yet. I'll write to you, and I'll expect to get a letter from you in return."

"That much I can promise," I said. "You will hear from me."

Mrs. Collingsworth told Paul to have a good trip and she'd see him at Christmas if not before. "Drive carefully now."

Once again the Flier was right on time. The conductor helped Mrs. Collingsworth onto the train and handed her her overnight case. She turned and waved and then disappeared into the Pullman car.

I told Dev she could take her mother back to the house and then just go on to the store. I'd pick Betsy up later.

There was one more thing to be done. I had to say something to Mrs. Skinner, and what could I say to this woman I'd been on cozy, girl to girl, terms with for a month and who now remembered none of it?

"It was good to meet your friend," I said, almost forgetting myself and calling her Cora.

"It was nice having her here," she said quietly. "We were always very close. I'm sure you will enjoy being with her when you go back there to school."

So Mrs. Skinner expects me to go too. No one was against it. There was Neena yet, but Mrs. Collingsworth seemed to think she knew how Neena would vote. I didn't respond to Mrs. Skinner's comment. Instead I shook her hand and said, "You stay well now." If she only knew the importance of that request.

She smiled at me and said she'd be fine.

Paul wished Dev good luck and told her and Mrs. Skinner he'd get to Bannister again. Next time he'd be able to find The Hill on his own.

Finally, he and I were the only ones left. We took my stuff back to the folks' house—funny how all at once I thought of it that way—*the folks' house.* I didn't really belong there anymore. If I had learned one thing through this whole experience it was that.

There didn't seem to be anybody home. We set my bag down just inside the door and came back out to the swing.

"I'm sorry to be leaving," Paul said, "but I don't have to be in Tucson until August. Maybe I'll come back after Durango. You're bound to have another rainstorm. I'll watch the forecasts. Besides, I think you'll wind up in Evanston. You'd be crazy not to."

"Okay, I'm crazy," I said just to end it.

At last Paul got to his feet and pulled me up to him. He's going to kiss me I thought, and I felt the goose bumps rise on my arms again. But he didn't. He just held both my hands and said very earnestly, "Don't forget me."

I think I was disappointed. I'm not sure. A kiss from Paul this soon might not be the best thing. I could wait. What I said was, "Who could forget the Mayor of Lodi? And honestly now, that's a great line. Where did you get it?"

"I'll never tell," he said, winking at me. "It's a family secret." And he strode down the walk.

He didn't turn around and I just stood there thinking what an intriguing guy this was. "Family secret." Okay. Maybe . . . Maybe . . . Just maybe, I will go to Evanston.

Once again **Virginia Bradley** draws on her Midwest background and captures the flavor of life in a small Nebraska town of the thirties. It was with her first young adult novel, *Bend to the Willow,* that the stage was set for the Mayor of Lodi.

Mrs. Bradley now lives in Santa Monica, California, where she is active as a literary consultant and a director of writing workshops. She is also the author of three collections of original plays for children which established her as a popular dramatist for young people.